Dad wrote
G L B

LAST DANCE!

She knew how to wheedle. "Mr. Slocum, to do what I ask, I'll pay you not one, but two silver cartwheels. Please? I wouldn't plead, but my life with Cecil St. James is over. I can't bear another day!" Slocum was about to give in. But just then: Ca-rar-*rack*! The sharp echoing report of a rifle rang out.

Fiona staggered back, hammered by an invisible fist. "Slocum, I'm hit," she croaked weakly.

Slocum spun on his heel, and saw the smoke puff hovering above the ambusher's blufftop position. He grabbed the woman and crabbed sidelong, his hand streaking for his six-gun . . .

THE BENT BOOK
90,000 Paperback Books
Trade 2 for 1
Buy at 60% of retail.
5055 B Memorial Drive
Stn., Mtn., Ga. 30083
292-4069

DON'T MISS THESE
ALL-ACTION WESTERN SERIES
FROM THE BERKLEY PUBLISHING GROUP

THE GUNSMITH by J. R. Roberts
   Clint Adams was a legend among lawmen, outlaws, and ladies. They called him . . . the Gunsmith.

LONGARM by Tabor Evans
   The popular long-running series about U.S. Deputy Marshal Long—his life, his loves, his fight for justice.

LONE STAR by Wesley Ellis
   The blazing adventures of Jessica Starbuck and the martial arts master, Ki. Over eight million copies in print.

SLOCUM by Jake Logan
   Today's longest-running action Western. John Slocum rides a deadly trail of hot blood and cold steel.

ASPEN BOOK SHOP
100,000 HARDBACKS, PAPERBACKS, NEW AND USED
CD'S, COMICS, RECORDS,
TRADE 2 FOR 1 EVERYTHING DISCOUNTED
6988 MEMORIAL DRIVE 296-3933

JAKE LOGAN

SLOCUM AND THE
COW TOWN KILL

BERKLEY BOOKS, NEW YORK

If you purchased this book without a cover, you should be aware that this book is stolen property. It was reported as "unsold and destroyed" to the publisher, and neither the author nor the publisher has received any payment for this "stripped book."

SLOCUM AND THE COW TOWN KILL

A Berkley Book / published by arrangement with
the author

PRINTING HISTORY
Berkley edition / June 1994

All rights reserved.
Copyright © 1994 by The Berkley Publishing Group.
This book may not be reproduced in whole or in part,
by mimeograph or any other means, without permission.
For information address: The Berkley Publishing Group,
200 Madison Avenue, New York, New York 10016.

ISBN: 0-425-14255-8

BERKLEY®
Berkley Books are published by The Berkley Publishing Group,
200 Madison Avenue, New York, New York 10016.
BERKLEY and the "B" design
are trademarks of Berkley Publishing Corporation.

PRINTED IN THE UNITED STATES OF AMERICA

10 9 8 7 6 5 4 3 2 1

SLOCUM AND THE
COW TOWN KILL

1

Crossing southeast Colorado on horseback in July, Slocum knew to expect the heat could be bothersome. After all, he'd spent the recent weeks in the Rockies, at elevations upward of two miles, depending on the mining camp. But already this day had stoked up hotter than the devil's griddle, and it wasn't even the middle of the morning. That's why he wasn't pushing the hardy, short-coupled roan he'd been straddling since sunup.

The man's dusty, trail-grimed clothes were glued with sweat to his big frame—height six feet and an inch, standing in his battered mule-ear boots. And he swayed in the saddle with the identical straight bearing as when he'd set out, partly from habit instilled when he'd served in the military, partly owing to his being a natural-born horseman.

Now the man kicked the flanks of his mount, urging it up yet another of the innumerable swells in the sun-cured dun plain. On topping the rise, he could see little change, just more of the same vast, empty terrain he'd been trailing south across for days.

Slocum scrubbed his sun-browned hand across a squarish jaw darkened by a three-day beard stubble, then stretched to pat the gelding's damp neck. "Keep up the good work, fella. Down to Socorro, where we're bound, it's a far piece, sure, but—"

As the rider's voice trailed off, the gelding just kept going as before. The mount, acquired by Slocum just before pulling out of Leadville, had served him well. Fifteen hands tall, it had a fairly deep chest in addition to strong and well-shaped legs, which translated into endurance.

And the endurance, in turn, had turned the recent days into good ones of covering distance: forty-five miles or so apiece, starting at sunup and riding through, with but few rests, until the darkness fell.

Tomorrow, Slocum reckoned, he should be crossing the line—finally—into New Mexico Territory.

Not that he disliked Colorado; the place had its good points. For example, just last week in the hectic atmosphere of booming Leadville, he'd managed to gamble his way up from stone broke, playing poker with three lucky-at-finding-minerals, *un*lucky-at-cards prospectors. And when he'd run up his stake, he'd had the sense to *pull* stakes, before he lost it all again. A wise move that Slocum was still congratulating himself for.

Now the country to the south beckoned, where he figured to take up an old friend's offer to go partners on a small horse-raising spread.

But that would only come about after still more days of grueling horseback travel. For the time being the big man simply rode, his form a mere speck on the landscape, a few hawks coasting above on wind currents—ones about as random as Slocum's life up till now. A funny thing, how up in Leadville it had come to him that it might be time to take up Billy Linn's offer, try his hand at settling down in the shadow of the looming natural monument Wild Horse Butte.

Oh, it would be quite a change, quitting the wandering life after years of playing a lone hand, dodging trouble at every turn, all over the West. He felt so good about the prospect, he actually whistled a few bars of a tune.

The sky was a vaulting azure dome, and underfoot buffalo grass spread between the distant hills like a wide, dry sea. The day wasn't so bad after all, Slocum decided, scanning about with eyes squinted half-shut against the sun's bright glare.

At least the major Indian threats were things of the past, and he had no worry of arrows from the bows of raiding Cheyenne or Kiowa. Which had been the chief pain in the ass of riding hereabouts in the bad old days . . .

Then, quicker than a blink of his alert, green eyes, the day's peace was broken. A sound—an alarming sound—reached Slocum's ears from some distance off. He swiveled his head, his senses straining.

Hadn't it been a scream that he'd heard? The scream of a frightened woman?

Slocum's wariness—as much part of him as the Colt Peacemaker riding in his cross-draw rig—was increased tenfold.

Scanning the broken ground off to his right, he spied the trouble. About a quarter mile off, a wildly rocking top buggy tore across a flat, the leggy bay mare in the shafts out of control and galloping full tilt. The reins were loose and flying, and that could spell only one thing: a runaway. The lone occupant of the rig was jouncing perilously on the sprung seat, hanging on for dear life.

Though there were shadows thrown by the conveyance's raised top, Slocum could tell that the person was a woman. The long, flaming hair, the skirts that billowed in the breeze of passage told him that.

But the man couldn't tell much more, not at a distance.

Giving spur to his mount, he sought to close that distance.

Slocum reined toward the broken stretch raced over by the buggy, and soon the roan was flying along in pursuit, gaining on the conveyance. The running buggy nag plunged up one hummock and down the next, jounced over bumps, threatening to overturn the rig. As Slocum drew closer, he could see the animal's foaming mouth, the eyes walling in its head, the wildly tossing mane. He could see something else: that the woman wasn't merely well-attired in a fine, flounced dress, a stylish hat perched on her head—she was good-looking. Damned good-looking!

Now she glanced over her shoulder and spotted the overtaking rider. "Help me!" she screeched. The red hair whipped about her pale, strained face. The woman's voice, blown by the wind, was tinged by panic.

On the buggy sped, as if Satan were at the mare's heels. Now the horse veered into a terrain of brush thickets, gullies, a snaking creek that flowed between sometimes-steep banks. And beyond those loomed an outcrop-studded bluff. The rig shot down a grade and splashed through the stream's shallows, its spinning wheels flinging jets of silvery water. But although the conveyance dragged by the runaway swayed crazily, it didn't slow.

Slocum spurred his surging roan alongside. Mesquite tangles rose to the right and the left, taloning branches raking the big man.

"Hang on, lady!" he called. "Hang on!"

The woman had no chance to answer, for a buggy wheel struck a rock and was slammed askew. The bay mare stumbled and screamed in terror, then crashed to earth, kicking and thrashing in its tangled traces. The buggy, careening into a cutbank, lurched to a stop.

It came to rest with the front end sharply uptilted. The woman tumbled off, landing in a heap.

Slocum stepped from leather and came running up.

"You all right?"

"Oh-h-h, . . . Tarnation!"

For the moment the woman was helpless, arms and legs flailing, skirts and frothy petticoats a messy tangle. "Can't you help me . . . up?" Slocum grabbed her arm and hauled her upright, seeing in her face now more frustration and less fear.

Which he understood, the threat to her life being over.

What he didn't understand was why she was scolding *him*.

"Just look at this mess!" the woman blurted. "My buggy, my horse! Mister, I do hope you're satisfied!"

"Me? What did *I* do?"

"Well, for one thing, you let the mare run down into this awful place. If you'd headed her off, kept her on the flat—"

Slocum raised his hand. "The horse was a runaway, lady. Do I guess right, that it got spooked by a rattlesnake?"

She pouted, but gave a nod. "Well, *I* certainly wasn't to blame!"

"So, it not being your fault, it must be mine?"

She used her slender hands to slap powdery, saffron dust from her dress—or try to. Only at last, when she stopped and looked up at Slocum, did her frown break. The woman smiled—and what a smile! Sizing her up at close range, Slocum found himself drinking in aquamarine eyes reflective of intelligence, fine-boned features, and flawless, milky skin. The dress of sky-blue dimity tapered to a narrow waist, above which the bodice was pushed out amply. She was a voluptuous woman, in her prime—if a woman's prime could be said to extend to her late thirties.

To Slocum's way of thinking, it could. She was of an age much to be appreciated, he'd been thinking for years now: old enough to be not only skilled, but grateful.

She laughed, if ruefully. "You're right," she admitted. "I'm sorry. You tried to save my life, and for that my thanks." She extended her hand. "My name is Fiona St. James, Mr.—?"

"Call me Slocum," he said. "John Slocum. You live near here, Miss St. James?"

"It's 'Mrs.,' I'm afraid." The smile faded like a frost-nipped blossom. "As for more about myself, Mr. Slocum, shouldn't we be dealing with first things first? Browny, my mare, she seems to be suffering."

She took a step toward the fallen animal, but Slocum intervened. "Don't go close. You might get kicked." He went on, explaining: "She may once have been a good horse, but now she's finished. That foreleg's broken above the fetlock—see?" His hand drifted to his holstered Colt. "That was the reason I asked if your home's nearby. On account of I need to—"

Fiona St. James blanched. "Put poor Browny out of her misery? Oh, Lord!" One milk-white hand wrung the other, which called Slocum's attention to her many jeweled rings. He'd seen the like only a few times, and that had been in high-toned places—like Denver's Windsor Hotel, or a mansion in San Francisco's Nob Hill section. Fiona St. James, in addition to diamonds, wore a glittering ruby, a glittering opal, and an eye-size pearl.

A rich woman, *and* fine-looking?

"Afraid so, ma'am," Slocum said about the mare.

She was clearly distressed, but said, "Oh, go ahead. Do what's required. I'll be waiting over there, under that tree."

Slocum drew his Colt, his fist wrapping the walnut buttplates of the heavy .44-40. The horse was lying there with pain-dulled eyes. Slocum eared the hammer back, pointed the gun at its head, and triggered. There was a crisp *crack,* and the horse shuddered, then died, voiding a rush of excrement.

Slocum stood in the sun, plugged a fresh round into his six-gun, then holstered the weapon. Next he drew a muslin tobacco sack and rolling papers from his shirt pocket and built himself an expertly handmade cigarette. It would have to do—last night in camp he'd finished the last of his cigars, the thin Havanas he favored. Now he thumbnailed a lucifer and fired up the quirly, inhaling a lungful of smoke and exhaling a bluish cloud. Trudging back to where his roan stood rein-thrown, he grasped the bridle to lead the animal. Having run as hard and willingly when called on, Slocum reckoned, it deserved the chance to do its grass cropping in pleasant shade.

Under a spreading cottonwood on the stream bank, the woman was pacing up and down, up and down. At his approach, she turned her somber face to him. "I'll be all right, Mr. Slocum. The matter of shooting Browny? I know it had to be done."

"Ma'am, it did. Now, about this fix you're finding yourself in—"

It was her turn to interrupt. "Let *me* say something first, John Slocum—please. I've a proposition I'd like to put to you."

He dragged on his smoke and met her gaze. "You know, somehow I guessed there'd be."

He'd been speculating on how she'd choose to handle it: tell him she just wanted to go home, or go someplace else? Although she was obviously well heeled, she wore a strangely edgy look . . .

"Mr. Slocum, you'll note my luggage in the buggy." She pointed, and yes, he saw the valise, the several gladstone bags. "I'm leaving my husband," she continued. "Yes, I'm actually on my way right now. Cecil and I haven't been getting along for quite some time. Before the accident just now, I was driving to Antelope Creek, a little town south of here. From there a stagecoach line runs back east."

"You're planning to catch a stage?"

A determined nod. "I can't go back to the Diamond 7. I simply can't." She gestured off to the west, presumably the direction of the spread she was talking about.

"Diamond 7? That your husband's ranch?"

"No. *My* ranch. My cattle. My house. All mine."

"But—"

She put her hand out and touched his sleeve. "Mr. Slocum, don't ask me to explain now. Later, perhaps— time is wasting. Antelope Creek is about a three-hour drive from here."

"That so?"

"I'm not just begging for you to help without reward. I intend to pay you—and I assure you, I am able to pay." She patted a kid-gusseted buck purse that she'd been clutching since falling from the buggy. "Here's my plan, Mr. Slocum. Aside from a paint scratch or two, the buggy looks undamaged. There's just the matter of getting it pulled out of that bank and turned around—"

"Suppose we manage it, lady. You're not going anyplace. You've got no horse."

The smile brightened still more. "Ah, but *you* have one! And you're a big, strong fellow, Mr. Slocum, able to drag dead Browny out of the traces. As soon as your roan is between the shafts, we can start, hopefully to reach Antelope Creek by dark. Did I mention some friends are expecting me? I plan to spend the night with them, catch the stage heading back east tomorrow. Mr. Slocum, to do what I ask, I'll pay you—" She hesitated for just a second. "I was going to say one, but make it two silver cartwheels?"

To Slocum, it was a worthwhile sum. Still: "But, money's not the only thing. You see, I'm heading on down toward Socorro—"

"Please? I wouldn't plead, Mr. Slocum, but my life with Cecil St. James is over. I can't bear another day!"

She knew how to wheedle—and Slocum was about to give in. But money wasn't the only reason: Between the time they left for town and their arrival, he'd have three whole hours to ply his woman-winning charms. Persuade Fiona not to stay with friends, but rather with "Gentleman John" Slocum in the best damned hotel the town had to offer . . .

But just then: Ca-rar-*rack*! The sharp, echoing report of a rifle rang out.

Fiona staggered back as if hammered by an invisible fist. "Slocum, I'm hit," she croaked weakly.

Slocum spun on his heel and saw the smoke puff hovering above the ambusher's blufftop position.

As he grabbed the woman and crabbed sidelong, his hand streaked for his six-gun.

2

Slocum hauled out his Peacemaker, brought it up, and—
to give the bushwhacker on the bluff something to worry
about—tossed a shot his way. Then he was scrambling
again toward the protection of the nearest boulder jumble,
one arm supporting the slumping form of Fiona St. James.

But then several things happened at once: first the woman
he clutched began to tremble badly. Glancing down, he saw
her face go ghastly white. The front of the blue dress now
glistened wetly crimson, and some of her blood had leaked
onto Slocum's shirt.

As if this weren't enough, another shot rent the air, and
behind him Slocum heard a shrilling neigh of pain. He spun
and saw his roan's legs fold and send the animal down.
He grasped the situation in a flash: The sniper's bullet had
missed hitting *him*, but had drilled into the eye of the horse,
killing it. It was dead before it hit the earth.

Now Slocum, in among the boulders, snapped off two
more shots at the sniper's position—or former position.
No bushwhacker in his right mind was likely to stay put,
he well knew. And if the bastard moved to again target his
victims, he could open up at any time, and dangerously.

In the baking silence of the sun-drenched coulee, Slocum
fed his Colt rounds. On the ground beside him lay Fiona,
unconscious and bloody. He knew he needed to stop the
bleeding or she'd die. He lifted and propped the woman

against a boulder. Her head sagged forward, spilling her hair, but Slocum swept aside the auburn cascade to fumble with Fiona's buttons. His big, blunt fingers popped a few.

Finally he resorted to tearing the fabric, exposing large breasts that under other circumstances would have drawn his eager hands. Now, however, the right globe displayed an ugly hole from which blood flowed in frequent spurts. And the exit hole in her back would be still worse, unless Slocum missed his guess.

Fiona's pierced chest rose and fell irregularly, but at least she was still breathing.

Then all at once, under his hands, the woman gave a frightful shudder. Pink foam spewed from Fiona's lips, and her body seemed to draw in on itself.

Just like that, she'd gone from living to dead.

Goddamn that bushwhacker!

Slocum laid the corpse back gently, then crawled to peer up between rocks at the gunman's ridge.

The shooter spotted him and fired, and Slocum's hat kited off to snag in a mesquite bush.

Slocum took a chance and sprinted for a nearby cottonwood clump, into which he dove headfirst. Then he bellied forward through spindly trunks, his .44 held clear of dust and grit. When he reached the edge of the trees, he was fairly close to the bluff, able to see the best way up its face, via what appeared to be a crooked game trail. Up he bounded and started to run, soon slogging over poor footing on a talus slope, then gaining the path, where he was concealed from up top.

At least that was what he thought for a brief moment.

But then a bullet spanged a boulder and sent hot lead ricocheting past his ear. Slocum forged on, legs pumping harder than before. The going was rough, and he was panting. The trail petered out, but Slocum kept on, soon arriving at the edge of the bluff's rounded, granite cap. He found a handhold and heaved himself up, then scooted toward a narrow niche between two standing rocks.

The reverberations of the gunplay were as dead as the woman he'd left back down below. Slocum crouched in his hole-up, the silence around him desolate, nerve-wracking.

When he finally moved, it was with care, squirming along the rock like an overgrown snake, attempting to shield himself from view of the ambusher. When he heard the click of metal on metal—a jingling spur?—he knew he was close. Fisting his Colt, he decided to make his play, since his unknown foe was on the other side of a bulging outcrop.

Slocum bolted from cover, then threw himself and rolled. A man whom he glimpsed fleetingly—silhouetted against a backdrop of blinding sun's glare—triggered his rifle. Lead zipping past him, Slocum fired also, one of his bullets striking the other man's bootheel, shattering it. Yelping, the man turned and bolted down a slope, limping wildly.

"Stop and shoot it out like a man, yellow belly!"

Slocum, on his feet again, gave pursuit over the stone-strewn ground. The pursued man ducked into a cedar bosquet, bulled through to the tune of much branch crashing. Seeking to head his quarry off, Slocum left the crest, leaping to a lower ledge and loping along it.

A man with his face mostly concealed by his wide brim appeared on the path, but on catching sight of Slocum, he turned and hurried off downslope, still gimping. Slocum tried to close in, but in vain: Before he'd gone ten yards more, he heard the clatter of hooves, and a horse broke from the trees, its rider spurring and rein whipping.

"Son of a bitch!"

The bastard—whose face he hadn't even gotten a good look at—was out of range.

Swearing softly, Slocum retraced his steps to where Fiona's body lay outstretched, empty, filmed eyes still fixed upward at the sky. He looked down at the dead woman and solemnly wagged his head.

She was rid of her husband now, but no better off.

Unless the grave had consolations Slocum didn't know about.

It was a quarter hour later, and Slocum stood between the dead woman and the dead roan. He reached out and retrieved his Stetson from a branch, noting the placement in the crown of the fresh bullet hole. It was in front and conspicuous, but he'd be damned if he'd discard the head-gear.

It seemed he had a feast of choices. The first decision—whether to hang around or start hiking—he made quickly. He'd be best off away from this place. Next, he'd need a destination—and two came to mind. There was the town of Antelope Creek, off to the south, and there was the Diamond 7 cattle spread, off to the west, the direction Fiona had pointed.

Two things mitigated against the town. One was the known quantity of distance: Fiona had called it a three-hour buggy ride. Hiking it would take at least twice the time. And then he'd need to buy a new mount, which would deplete his funds. And when he'd looked in Fiona's handbag and luggage, he'd found no money at all.

So much for her "ability to pay" for services rendered. True, she might have owned a bank account, but that did Slocum no good now. By now he was plenty sore over this whole affair, which, aside from nearly getting him shot, had put him out of pocket the price of a horse.

So who had shot the woman? The husband, Cecil, as he recalled her calling him?

To Slocum the killing of Fiona was remarkable for its cold-bloodedness, the result of a determined stalk followed by a display of sound marksmanship. Slocum realized he lacked the knowledge of whether Cecil St. James possessed the needed rifle skills.

Fiona had spoken of her husband to Slocum only briefly.

But she'd spoken of nobody else at all—at least, not specifically. Those friends of hers in town had to be assumed to be just that: friends and not enemies. And when conversing with Slocum after the excitement of the runaway, she hadn't seemed afraid for her life—not as if she were worried over being stalked, then murdered.

Slocum was no Pinkerton, but he could put two and two together. The ranch belonged to Fiona, and Fiona had been in the process of walking out on Cecil—presumably leaving him with nothing. So, what was Cecil to think, if he'd married for money and the money was about to be cut off?

"Ah, 'murder most foul,' " sighed Slocum. Once in Deadwood he'd attended a performance of a Shakespeare play, and the phrase had stuck. But dead poets aside—was he forced to be the goat in this mess? Lose a good horse because a man had killed, trying to hold onto an easy life?

Hell, no!

So that much was decided: He'd go to the ranch—afoot—and confront Cecil St. James. By leveraging the widowed rancher, he stood to gain a replacement of the dead roan. Or money. Or both—to make up for his being inconvenienced.

Now all that remained here was to pile a few rocks on Fiona to discourage the buzzards, coyotes, and other scavengers. Slocum took it for granted that the dead woman wouldn't be left out here for long—not after he'd spread the word of what had happened. With a woman like Fiona—rich and all—there'd likely be a host of friends and relatives to provide a decent funeral and burial.

Slocum's last decision was really no decision. He wasn't going to abandon his saddle, a broken-in Visalia-tree steel-fork with twin California white-hair cinches. Or his twenty-inch barrel carbine, a nicely sighted-in Winchester '73.

He strode to the dead roan and stripped his gear, then filled his canteen at the creek, upstream from where Browny had bled and shit her last.

It was a half hour or so later when, saddle rig chewing his shoulder, Slocum started walking. Following the tracks made by Fiona's buggy was easy enough. But Slocum had no clue as to how far off the ranch called the Diamond 7 was.

Fiona hadn't mentioned that.

With his luck, Slocum thought, it figured to be a good long way.

"Shit," Slocum grumbled, trudging.

The afternoon dragged for Slocum as he slogged on west, following the buggy tracks. His saddle, saddlebags, and blanket rode one broad shoulder; his canteen swung from the other on a thong. His left hand hefted his trusty Winchester, and the weight of the long gun made his load top out at more than sixty pounds.

The sun was a lemon-yellow eye, flinging down heat and dazzle, seemingly alive in its intensity. Slocum was sweating from every pore, and had been since leaving the coulee, buggy, dead woman, and dead horses. Ahead, the tan buffalo-grass rolled away, the vista horizon-wide and numbingly monotonous. But the tracks he followed were perfectly clear in the soft earth, giving him no concern that he'd miss the Diamond 7, should it be off in some concealed valley or box canyon.

Recalling the spooked buggy horse, he kept an eye peeled for rattlers. He occasionally saw one, but there was little other life in this sere land, unless you counted the flies, the jackrabbits, and the soaring hawks that sailed the high, metallic sky.

But Slocum doggedly kept up his pace, occasionally shifting the heavy saddle. After the first number of miles, his feet were feeling the strain, due both to their not being

used to long hikes, and to his lack of wisdom back when
he'd bought his footgear. He'd selected the cowman's boots
for style, not appropriateness for walking. The ache in
Slocum's legs and ankles turned to pain; blisters rose inside
the offending boots, then broke. His socks were wet and
squishy, and not only from sweat.

And as for sweat, there was his soaked-through shirt,
by now clinging and abominably itchy. John Slocum—as
the miles unfolded—was sunbaked, footsore, and fuming.
Most of his curses were for Cecil St. James, whom he held
responsible.

Either the husband or someone the husband had hired—
good bets to have killed Fiona. Slocum rather doubted
he'd recognize the culprit if he ever saw him again. But
even if Cecil or Cecil's man had fired from that bluff, the
husband had driven the wife from home. That act had put
her alongside Slocum—at a terribly wrong time in a very
deadly wrong place.

Damn it, he'd see his horse replaced! He naturally
assumed the Diamond 7's remuda was well stocked.

When he came in sight of the cluster of ranch buildings,
Slocum estimated he'd come about ten miles. Ten miles,
and he was hobbling! As Slocum made his way down
into the shallow, slope-walled canyon that enclosed the
headquarters site, the sun had scaled well down the western
sky, but there was plenty of daylight yet.

Approaching, he saw the spread—a sprawling affair, complete with a pole-arched gate to the yard, strong corrals for
horses and other livestock, sheds and barns—and, beyond the
barns, fenced grassy pastures. Slocum saw bunches of cattle
on the far flats, but his eyes were drawn primarily to the
main ranch house, a mansion—although not of any particular architectural style. The rambling house was part adobe,
part logs, with gables facing various directions, many windows on both lower and upper stories. An L-shaped veranda
ran along two sides, and the whole was splashed—in late

afternoon—with golden sunlight.

The spread was a beehive of activity, as punchers moved about the yard at an assortment of tasks. To Slocum a good number of horses in the corrals looked good, but he decided not to consider any of the raw ones, those still under the jurisdiction of a bronc peeler. Slocum hiked past several bastionlike outcroppings, through the main gate and into the yard, where he was finally noticed. When alongside a water trough he let down saddle and gear, the ranch hands started ambling up, inspecting him from under their wide ranchmen's hat brims.

Slocum spoke first: "This spread's the Diamond 7?"

"Yeah, it is—"

But the first cowpoke to speak was shoved aside. His place was taken by a tall drink of water wearing a Dakota-creased Stetson, hard of muscle and hard of face. Hard of voice, too, when he started to talk. "State your business, stranger," the man demanded.

"You know," Slocum said, "somehow you don't look like a Mr. St. James. I'd just as soon do my palavering with the boss."

"I'm the boss."

"Fella, you're the ramrod, by your look. Hell, lookit the horseshit on your boots."

A harder looking of Slocum up and down. "What you say your name is, mister?"

"I'm not shy. Call me Slocum."

More punchers kept gathering, something Slocum didn't like, but which he was powerless to remedy. None of the men looked too friendly, and most packed six-guns—but then, this *was* rattler country. The hands that concerned Slocum most were holding tools; for example a blacksmith clutched a hammer—a big hammer. Others fisted hayforks, and one even a coiled bullwhip.

"Slocum, hey?" someone drawled. "Boys, any of y'all know a Slocum?"

"Naw."

"Naw."

"I thought not." The lean man now sneered and wagged his jaw. His unblinking cat's eyes might have intimidated some, but not Slocum.

"So, Reeve, you gonna run him off?" The speaker was a runty puncher with a feral face.

"Kick his tail, maybe?" the blacksmith quipped. The man's shoulders were nearly as wide as a shed door, and the rope-like muscles in his heavy arms twitched. He'd be hard to handle, Slocum felt. Even if he weren't clutching that dangerous-looking hammer.

"Look, gents," he tried again. "Call Cecil St. James out. No reason for trouble."

"No reason but *you*."

"Who y'think y'are? A badass?"

"Draggin' in here, a no-account saddle tramp—"

It was inevitable: Somebody remarked on Slocum's side-arm. "Lookit his gun rig, fellas! Ass-backwards, b'gawd! Oughtn't we take it, ram it down the bastard's throat?"

Slocum's gaze roamed beyond the crew, and he noticed, in the window of the big house, the shadow of a watching person. A curtain that had been pulled back dropped into place. But who'd been watching, the owner of the spread? Or the cook? A Mexican or an Indian servant?

"Look, if you want a fight," Slocum drawled, "how about a one-on-one? Shit, I'll stash my hogleg, take on Reeve, there, with my fists—"

His hands were at his gunbelt. He might be willing to unbuckle and drop it; he might not. He knew there was no assurance he'd be allowed a fair fight, and none but a fool would take on a crowd of hostile stompers.

Slocum hated mincemeat, and not only in pies.

"Fight you, Slocum? I wouldn't dirty my hands," the man called Reeve spat. "The spread's champ rough-and-tumble battler, he's Dutch Mueller, here."

"Mueller where?"

"Right in front of you. Wearin' the leather apron!"

The blacksmith? *Uh-oh!*

Slocum's hand poised near his Colt, but he saw he was covered—by a dozen six-guns, at least. He tossed his hat down, then unbuckled his cartridge belt and holstered Colt. He let the rig down gently atop the hat, protecting it somewhat from the deep dust that lay everywhere.

"All right, gents," Slocum announced. "Mueller, he can try me if he's of a mind to. The fight will be no-holds-barred, I reckon? Of course, I'm just guessing what you boys might want to be treated to."

Mueller had shed his apron, baring a hairy barrel chest. Muscles slabbed his brawny torso, making him look top-heavy. So, how many pounds did he have on Slocum? Fifteen? Twenty? The smith bared brown, crooked teeth, but he was snarling, not grinning.

"I'm a-gonna pound out your lights, pilgrim," he whooped.

Dutch charged Slocum with his tree-limb arms up and flailing.

3

Slocum watched the charging giant called Mueller coming at him. He bunched his fists and rose on his toes to meet the onslaught.

At least the blacksmith had handed off the hammer he'd been armed with; a man standing next to Reeve was holding the tool.

Growling and chuffing, Mueller closed with his slighter, hike-fatigued opponent. Slocum dodged the first free-swinging roundhouse blow, but the second grazed his shoulder, partially numbing it.

Thrown off balance, he sought to recover, but was punished by a punch, this time to his chest. *Damn!* His reflexes were dulled by fatigue, his legs tight from the ten-mile walk he'd just been through. But determined to bounce back, he threw a punch that slammed the smith's breastbone.

Mueller, unfazed, roared his fury and waded in again with fists swinging.

This time Slocum feinted with his right hand and shot out his left, to impact with a blunt Germanic jaw. Dutch's head snapped back, and then, eyes darting flames like twin lucifers, the man leapt forward. A missed uppercut fanned Slocum's face, but the follow-up—which connected with his cheek—jarred him to the soles. Shaking off the fireworks spinning in his brain, Slocum backpedaled. The leering, brutal smith shuffled after him.

Shouts of encouragement rang in the air of the Diamond 7 yard, the crowd of punchers loudly backing their champ. Or the man they wanted to be their champ—Slocum was far from finished. He'd taken note of the way Mueller telegraphed his punches: a slight turn of the head, not much, but enough. With the smith's next body blow on its way, Slocum sidestepped, and let the bull-necked fellow come slogging after him.

Then, reversing himself and dancing in swiftly, Slocum drove both fists to bury themselves in the smith's heavily fleshed breadbasket.

The man doubled over, at the same time reeling back. The cheers of his backers turned to groans as the smith's wide rump hit the hardpan. But he was up again in a flash, heavy features dripping sweat.

"You grub-line son of a bitch—"

"Come and get me, Mueller. Or are you nothing but mouth, and full of shit at that?"

Dutch Mueller roared and made a diving lunge, but at that moment Slocum stepped in to lash out with his fists, putting full strength behind the blows. The smith was halted in his tracks, and stood staggering. Another feeble, panicky swing missed, and Slocum knew it was time to move in for the put-away. He powered his right around with a full-armed smash, connecting with chest and bringing his adversary's chin down.

Then he grabbed a handful of hair and positioned the ugly head. "Let me go, bastard!" squawked Mueller. "I'll rip out yer throat—!"

Slocum sledged a hook into the smith's jaw, driving the man back into a corral fence post. Mueller slouched into a sagging fall, pitched on his face in hoof-churned dust, and then was still.

Slocum turned to the foreman with a grim smile. "Now, Reeve, about me seeing your boss, Mr. St. James—"

"You dumb-luck saddle bum," yelped the foreman. "Drop him, boys! Nobody gets the better of ol' Diamond 7!"

What Slocum confronted now was a hostile, armed gang. From all sides men were closing in with hammers, wheel spokes, whip hafts, and the like. Hearing their chorus of curses, Slocum planted his feet, got ready . . .

"What's going on out here? Stop this, you men! *I say,* stop it!"

The punchers, like puppets with jerked strings, froze. Slocum peered around, not letting his guard down, and saw the speaker, a newcomer on the scene and an entirely different sort from what he'd just faced. This one wore a red-and-black-checked shirt of what looked like silk, and at his throat one of those necktie-like rigs Slocum knew were called ascots. His whipcord trousers—jodhpurs?— were stuffed into tall, black stovepipe boots with silver-mounted spurs affixed.

The man packed an ivory-handled Remington in a holster of fine, elaborately tooled cordovan, and completed the costume with a high-crowned, wide-brimmed Stetson. The hat, the color of cream, looked fresh from the mail-order box.

"Who have we got here, Reeve?" the owner snapped, his voice distinctive for its pronounced British accent.

"Fella name of Slocum, Mr. St. James." The formerly mean-faced ramrod was all courtesy toward his boss, the rancher. "This *hombre* walked in here, started talkin' bold as brass—"

"And you decided he should be put in his place?" Cecil St. James stamped his well-shod foot. "And decided that Mueller was the one to do the honors?"

"Yessir. Y'see—"

Turning to Slocum, St. James said, "Don't think I'm apologizing, or that I'm soft, my man. Neither is true, a fact inevitably learned by the dozens of tramps who present themselves here each year. I've no use for their sort, whether begging a free meal or a— Dear me! What's the American term? Ah, yes, I recall: a grubstake. But I *do* take pride in my sense of fairness—Marquis of Queensberry rules for boxing matches, the whole lot engaged in by a true sportsman. Which is why you should consider yourself lucky this afternoon, Mr. Slocum."

"Because you fancy yourself a decent bloke, St. James?"

A small, tight grin. "It isn't what I merely fancy, Slocum. It's what I *am*. But just now, on a whim, I'm permitting you to state your business. My only warning is this: Be brief. My housekeeper is engaged now in laying out my supper. When I happened to glance out the window and noticed the disturbance out here, I was about to smoke my before-meal pipe. If you talk fast, I may be able to enjoy one, still."

With the punchers standing about wearing sullen expressions, Slocum sized up their employer. There was no denying the Brit cut a figure, a distinguished-looking man in his prime, handsome, if a bit dandified. He wore his hair shoulder-length, George Armstrong Custer style—except in the rancher's case, it flowed in lustrous brown waves. The mustache was waxed, the cheeks and chin scrubbed pink, fresh-shaven.

St. James was an inch or so taller than Slocum, but wasn't as heavyset—not that a trace of weakness showed in his piercing eyes. Now they glared at Slocum from under down-at-the-corners eyelids that gave the owner a certain haughty look.

But Slocum wasn't cowed by family or position. Planting himself in front of Cecil, he said, "Oh, I'll come right to the point, St. James. It's this: The way I calculate it, you owe me a saddle horse to ride out of here on. I'm sure you noticed I came afoot onto Diamond 7 property." The Englishman wanted to speak, but Slocum cut him off. "I'll tell you the why of that in a minute. Just get used to the notion, while I pick up my gun and gunbelt, strap 'em back on."

With the gunbelt again around his waist, carefully adjusted to ride slightly above his hipbones, Slocum went on talking: "Prepare for bad news, St. James. Your wife, Fiona, is dead. I was with her this morning when she was killed."

"What? How—? Look here, man, this is no joking matter!"

Slocum frowned. "No call for you to doubt what I say. Think a minute. Is she here at the ranch? No, and I'll bet she hasn't been seen for hours."

"Well, that's true enough," St. James confirmed. "As it happens, Fiona packed some bags and drove off this morning in the trap behind a bay trotter—"

"I know. And she took no ranch hands to act as escorts— likely because they're used to working for you, not her. Well, we ran into each other, she and I, when I stopped her spooked and out-of-control nag. And while we stood jawing afterwards," Slocum snapped his finger, "just like *that,* she got shot by a man with a rifle. And now my problem is the same fella that killed your woman killed my mount."

St. James looked shocked—convincingly so. If he's an actor, Slocum thought, he's a good actor. As for the cowhands, they, too, seemed surprised. Several stared blankly; several mumbled and wagged their heads.

"The boss lady gunned down?"

"Whilst drivin' out, all by her lonesome?"

"Hell of a thing—"

Even Reeve managed to avoid appearing guilty.

St. James, his face gone pale, addressed Slocum: "Decent of you, old chap. I mean, to come here and tell us, considering you were cast afoot. I feel an apology is in order— my men have standing orders to run off drifters, and so would've fancied they were doing their jobs. But you've obviously had a grueling walk, and just to inform me of my poor wife's end."

Now Slocum's tight smile came back. "You've not got that quite right, St. James. Clean out your ears: I came because I need a horse. A good horse. The roan I lost was a sound animal, with good bottom and a smooth gait I'd gotten to like."

"I hardly think, my good fellow—"

"Oh, quit shilly-shallying! You must know what I'm driving at."

St. James stood stroking his long face. "Slocum, surely you see my shock. Where did the—er, crime happen? I take it the perpetrator made his escape?"

"Did the killer get away? Yeah. We traded shots, but it was no use—he had a horse waiting, and I had none by then. Where did it happen? I'll play along and say: You know a bluff above a stream back about a two-hour walk east?"

"Breadloaf Bluff? Of course we know it! Even though it's on the other side of the ranch boundary." St. James winced and slapped his forehead. "Good God, I just thought of something: Fiona's remains! Evening is coming on, and she—she's lying out there! Some of the men must take a buckboard and fetch her. You know, Slocum. I mean, of course, for burial, laying her to her last rest."

"The spot won't be hard to find," Slocum said. "I put the lady in a cut and piled on plenty of rocks to keep buzzards away. She's lying not too far from her buggy."

"Kyle," St. James snapped to Reeve, "take some of the hands and get right on this. I mean now!"

"Sure thing, Mr. St. James. We'll hitch up a rig, get horses saddled, and ride out pronto."

The ramrod hurried off with some men, but the others continued to stand around, confusion written on their features. Slocum told the Englishman, "St. James, what say we step out of the sun—onto the veranda, maybe? I see rocking chairs up there—"

"I understand if you need to take a load off your feet— No, that's not it? You want to talk privately to me? Yes, of course—there's something more about Fiona's death.

Something the ranch hands have no business hearing? Come along into the house."

As the two men turned away from the others, Slocum thought his suspicions had been confirmed. Nobody—St. James, Reeve, nobody—acted like he suspected yours truly, Slocum. Now, if that didn't smell fishy . . .

Slocum and St. James strode toward the mansion. The murder rankled Slocum, but he wasn't a lawman.

He really should be getting down to Socorro . . . Shouldn't he?

None of this was any of his business, really . . . Was it?

4

Inside the parlor of the rambling mansion, Cecil St. James whipped off the big hat, to display a narrow, pinkish, mostly bald pate. He made a beeline for a sideboard of polished oak, where he slapped the headgear down and pulled out a foot-tall crystal decanter. "I need a drink, Slocum. You'll join me?"

"I reckon."

"Brandy or whiskey?"

"Whiskey."

"Good show." The Englishman splashed generous dollops of amber liquid into glass tumblers, then handed Slocum one. While St. James tossed off his shot, Slocum sipped slowly. It was excellent, years-old stuff, Slocum discovered, and it went down smooth as cream, lay in the stomach and smoldered with quiet authority. It was probably the best liquor Slocum had tasted all year.

Any drinking man would have approved of it.

He glanced around the interior of the room. Most folks of so-called good taste would likely have approved of *it*, Slocum sensed, although it was far from being a place where he himself could feel at ease. The entry hall, which they'd come through, was imposing, lit with muted colors from door-flanking stained-glass windows. As for this room, the parlor, it was expensively paneled in walnut, solid evidence of the wealth of the owner. The ceiling was plastered, the furniture fine mahogany chairs and divans, upholstered in damask or brocade, and protected with crocheted-silk antimacassars. There were narrow tables supporting lamps and china figures, and the walls held gilt-framed landscapes and a large French pier glass. There was a Brussels carpet on the floor, and a harmonium, complete with silver candlestick.

The fireplace at the far end of the room was tiled and had a marble mantel, and above it hung a gilt-framed portrait of a woman—a beautiful redhead in a velvet gown. The life-like image was of a young Fiona, and it seemed to Slocum that she was peering straight down at him. Afternoon sun filtered through the room's lace curtains, and rich oil colors gleamed in the soft light.

Overall, the room looked like money—plenty of money. Cecil St. James appeared a cultured man, and Slocum recalled how he'd behaved when first he'd laid eyes on him: superior, and bred to let it show. A member of some folderol English family? But Fiona had claimed everything belonged to her, nothing to her husband—not the ranch, the house, the herds, none of it.

A young woman of about eighteen—comely and Mexican, wearing a white maid's cap—thrust her head into the room. "Not now, Lupe, girl," St. James said, authority in his voice. "I and my guest, we're occupied." Eyes bright but not curious, she retreated. St. James turned back to Slocum. "Pardon my manners earlier, Slocum. My only excuse might be the position I'm in. This is the house. Fiona's design, Fiona's selection of furnishings. Excellent taste, what? She was quite a woman."

Slocum didn't mention that he'd been in finer places. The woodwork here was the work of craftsmen, true, but it could hardly compare to that of an Old South plantation house. Slocum's mind drifted to another time, the time of the War Between the States. Sergeant John Slocum, Army of the Confederacy, had been summoned to deliver a message from the hand of General Robert E. Lee . . .

No, the St. James's woodwork wasn't a century old, hadn't been waxed and rubbed over a span of years by a succession of diligent black servants.

"Yeah," Slocum said now. "Mrs. St. James. Quite a woman . . . that is, while still alive."

St. James turned from the painting and planted a buttock on a lamp table. "So, Slocum, she actually conversed with you? You say it happened after you stopped her runaway horse. Yes, she *would* chat with someone who saved her life—never mind his station." The aristocrat took another sip of the aged liquor. "Did my wife tell you about this ranch, how we bought it? We met, y'know, in Kansas, a place called Runnymede. In those days home to disgraced English knobs."

"That so?" Slocum fished out the makings and rolled a quirly, spilling a few tobacco grains. He fired up his smoke and deposited the extinguished lucifer in a potted palm.

"Quite right. Interesting place, Runnymede—founded by a man named Turnly. Oh, I'd been a wastrel in my youth, both in the Cotswolds, site of my family's estate, and up in London. No use denying my passion for racehorse gambling and chasing skirts. Was a cad, I'll admit, leading astray a baron's virgin daughter. So my father, Sir Reginald, shipped his youngest son off to America—the least embarrassing way out."

St. James went on: "As for Runnymede, it had a good tennis club, adequate polo. Rode to hounds in our scarlet coats, tally ho—but not *quite* the same as back in England. We hunted coyotes, not foxes, there being no red bush-tails in the Kansas countryside.

"But, Slocum, I digress. One fine day in Runnymede, Fiona Lewis stepped down from the stagecoach. She'd come to visit a friend, but I made dashing Cecil more fetching than old-flame Kip. Slocum, she belonged to the Massachusetts Lewises—you've heard of 'em? Textile mills, man! Textile mills! After merely a few weeks I popped the question. Thanks to luck, I made her my blushing bride."

Slocum tapped ashes into his emptied glass. "Let me get this straight—you were black sheep in a family of English blue bloods? Put to pasture in Kansas, but managed to marry a well-off wife?"

St. James laughed. "Supremely well-off! I say, Slocum! When Fiona's father died, his fortune came to her, all but small pittances to poor relations. It was then the notion struck us to move further west, enter the cattle business. Fiona and I got along famously—better than in recent years. Before all the squabbling—"

"You and Mrs. St. James," Slocum asked, "you didn't have kids?"

St. James shrugged. "No. Which now means no complicated inheritance. I'm sole heir."

"You mentioned you and your wife drawing apart. You took up with other women, right? Servant gals?"

A nod. "Beauties came along, and I didn't resist. Girls like Lupe, but not actually her. Lupe was Fiona's personal maid. I never stooped that-all low."

"Low, though?"

"*Rather.* More whiskey?"

"If you're offering."

St. James poured. "Playing the host, as a gentleman's taught. Actually, though, *I* need these drinks. Fiona dead! Gad!"

"You're surprised at her murder?"

"Why wouldn't I be?" The aristocrat's head came around; the mustache twitched. "But wait! I see where this leads! You're implying that I may have had something to do with her being shot. Now, look here, Slocum—"

The more Slocum thought, the clearer it was: The whole Diamond 7 ranch, plus other property, had belonged to Fiona. Cecil's liking for "a little on the side" had fostered resentment between husband and wife. Finally fed up, Fiona decided to walk, probably to consult with back-east lawyers about a divorce.

If the ranch had been sold from under Cecil, no confrontation would have been required. Everything might have gone nice and clean, as at some time the sheriff would have evicted the bloke.

If Cecil had seen it coming, he might have wanted his wife dead—and awaited his time. Slocum could relate to that: There were times when he, too, had exercised patience. He recalled a day in Texas, waiting out a Comanche renegade. He'd been trapped in a hole-up. Slocum had had more patience—and Slocum was the one who'd walked out alive.

Now he eyeballed the Englishman. Was he the size of the rifleman he'd chased? Nearly. Slocum swore under his breath, angry at having not seen the ambusher's face. As for clothing, St. James's was completely different. Also, no shot-up bootheel—but clothes could be changed. The Englishman had had time . . .

"Slocum, I didn't kill my wife! Say, what brought you here, anyhow? Have you to do with the law?" Bloodshot eyes looked Slocum up and down. "No, you don't look like law. You're a damned tough chap, though. You outfought Mueller, made him look puny."

Slocum had grown bored. Fiona was dead, and nothing would bring her back. She hadn't been close to Slocum or a Slocum friend, and the big man felt no particular vengeance bent. But he did need a horse, preferably a good one. Not a quick, short-run cow pony, but a deep-bottomed trail mount.

He'd seen the kind in St. James's corral. Several, in fact. He could maybe pick the size, the color . . .

"I want a horse, Cecil, remember? To replace the one I lost?"

"Why'd you come into the house? Oh, let me guess! You planned to wring me a bit, that's it? A bit of extortion?

Threatening to spread it around that I killed Fiona, then turning the screw." Suppressed rage lurked behind Cecil's bleary gaze. "But you're wrong, fellow! Dead wrong!"

Just then a woman glided into the room, the hem of her dress sweeping the waxed parquet. Her coal-black hair was tied back, Spanish-style, and her copper skin would have proclaimed her Mexican if that hadn't. "Señor St. James—"

"Yes, Yolanda? Dinner?"

"Sí."

"Slocum, my housekeeper, Yolanda. Yolanda, Mr. Slocum, here, brings bad news—bad and sad. Mrs. St. James has been killed, murdered while out in her carriage. Reeve and some men have gone out. They'll bring in her remains."

"I am sorry, sir." Still expressionless: a strange, mysterious woman.

To Slocum: "I say, old boy—let me convince you! Stay and eat? Yolanda, set another place at table."

Her hands smoothed her apron. "Sí." And then she was gone, having exited to the dining room.

"She's an excellent cook."

"Among other things?" Slocum questioned.

"Among other things."

"After the meal, we'll go out, pick my horse?"

"Bloody sod! Oh, all right, Slocum. I'll go to the corral with you."

Slocum grinned. "A meal would go well first, I admit. My backbone's tickling my belly button. I hope the meal's beef."

"Isn't this a cattle ranch? But with a fine vegetable plantation, of which I'm justly proud." St. James smiled, somewhat less bitterly. "A fine staff of Mexican gardeners. Trust me."

Slocum wasn't about to. Not as Fiona had done.

Slocum trailed the Englishman on in to dinner. He was betting he could look out for himself with St. James.

For the next hour or so, anyway.

5

Darkness washed the extensive Diamond 7 ranch yard, producing a thousand shadows from the buildings, the fences, the trees. Slocum, leaning his bulk against a fence rail, cast his eyes upward and saw a million or more stars. They hung in the vast, inky dome, glinting and winking, seemingly close enough to touch. He fished out the makings and slowly, methodically, went about building himself a quirly. Then he stood a while enjoying the warmth that still lay settled in his belly—his pleasantly full belly.

It had been a good meal, served by Lupe and an Indian gal called Alicia, a member of the Montana Flathead tribe. Lupe, of course, hailed from south of the Rio Grande.

So did Yolanda, Cecil had revealed to Slocum. Cecil, the genteel host, quick with precisely the correct soupspoon or salad fork, humorous banterer on dozens of light subjects.

The only subject St. James was no good with was Fiona. But the booze kept flowing for both the diners, and finally night had fallen. St. James had led the way on getting tipsy, and Slocum had followed—enough to take his mind off his sore feet. The Englishman begged off going to the corrals that night, claiming that the lanterns would not be bright enough to judge horseflesh by. Then he'd promised Slocum a good mount indeed, come morning, if he'd wait.

That was when pretty Lupe had entered the dining room, bearing desserts in quaint silver dishes. They were cherry tarts, Slocum found, and they tasted fine. Better than fine.

Another gulp from his brandy snifter, and Slocum had agreed to St. James's deal. Invited to sleep in a mansion guest room, he declined, explaining that he'd be more comfortable out under the stars. St. James told him his soogans were with his saddle in the tack shed, where they'd been stashed by a hand called Chuck.

While St. James staggered off upstairs on Yolanda's arm, Slocum had taken leave. Now he stood outside the tack shed. For bedding down, he liked the look of the nearby clump of cedars—nothing like fragrant fir needles to spread a man's bedroll on. Slocum was about to enjoy his last smoke of the day.

He heard the footsteps coming his way, but felt no danger. "Slocum," croaked a reedy voice. "That you?"

"Well, it's not the Marquis of Queensberry."

"Who?"

"Queensberry? Oh, he's a boxing expert one keeps hearing of from time to time. Seriously, yeah, I'm Slocum. Who are you, by the way?"

As he said this last, Slocum planted the quirly between his lips and scratched the lucifer on a fence post. In the match's flare, he made out his companion: a weather-beaten, lined old face, its lower half covered by scraggly gray beard. He recognized the man as one he'd seen that afternoon, part of the crowd who'd watched the fight with Mueller. "Who do I be, you wonderin'?" the old-timer mumbled, around a cheek-filling quid of Kentucky cut-plug. "Call me Wasatch, number one handyman on this spread. Used to be a proper top hand, but that was in bygone days. A fella ages and gets stove up—rheumatiz and such."

The match flickering out, Slocum drew in smoke and let it out through his nostrils. "Getting old happens, old-timer, to all of us, sooner or later."

Wasatch gestured with a gnarled hand. "The boys, they ain't back yet."

"The ones gone after Mrs. St. James? No, Wasatch, they aren't back. Reckon Kyle Reeve saw fit to take his time."

The old man spat tobacco juice, a portion of which contributed to staining his beard. "Figures. The ramrod, he's no prize. He never shoulda rousted you this afternoon. A fool coulda seed you ain't no troublemaker."

Slocum couldn't help liking the old man. "As to being a troublemaker? Maybe I really am sometimes. No hard feelings, Wasatch. Between us two, anyhow."

Wasatch, to rest his bones, perched on a pine-stump chopping block. "Watching that 'ere fight? Did some of us good, Slocum—lots of good. Seein' Mueller get his ass whupped. You sure can handle your fists, mister. Guns, too, I bet. I seen your rifle, and it's got that cared-for look."

"A man like me, a gun's his amigo."

A wheezing laugh. "And you got damned few other friends! Haw! A tough nut!"

Slocum grinned. Wasatch was all right, his instincts told him. "Since you're here, old-timer, you mind answering some questions?"

He scratched his pipestem neck. "For you? I reckon not."

"You been working long at the Diamond 7?"

"Since the St. James couple bought the spread. Place weren't much back then—nary a house, nary a barn. Nigh ten year ago, that was."

Slocum thought a minute. Then: "Reeve. How long has he been around here?"

"Oh, 'bout three-four year. Mr. St. James hired him, not the missus. Funny, Kyle allus seemed to like her so much—leastwise at first. Things did change later. Manuel Ramirez come, him and his wife, Yolanda."

"Yolanda, the housekeeper?"

"That's the one."

"Have I seen Manuel around?"

Another snort: "Ha! Manuel, one tall *hombre, muy*

vaquero? No, Slocum, you ain't seen him. He's dead. Buried over in the ranch plot." He gestured behind him, up the piney slope. "Funny, *she'll* get laid not far from him. May both of 'em rest in peace."

Slocum's curiosity was more idle than otherwise. In the morning, straddling his new horse, he'd ride out and not look back. And yet he asked it: "Wasatch, let me get this straight. Fiona St. James once liked Kyle Reeve, but then Kyle found his time beat by a dashing Mexican?"

A nod and spitting of brown juice. "C'rect!"

"And this Manuel Ramirez, he ended up dead?"

"Dead as a horseshoe nail. Last year. Bronc-stomped somethin' turrible."

Cagily: "Foul play—was there any involved?"

Wasatch finger-combed his beard—Slocum could hear faint *scritch-scritch* sounds. "Don't reckon there was foul play. O' course, them two didn't like him none—Kyle and St. James."

"Kyle was jealous over Ramirez, his attentions to Fiona? And St. James was the pissed-off husband—?"

"Why, hell no!"

"Huh?"

"Manuel carried him a plumb-hefty dong, he did. Followed the damn thing wherever it led him. From Miz St. James one night to Yolanda the next, and even an Injun maid or two—"

The impact of Wasatch's words dawned on Slocum. "Christ! St. James was jealous, then, on account of Yolanda!"

The old-timer looked sly. In the near-dark the big man could make out his eye whites. "Fine-lookin' yeller wench," Wasatch confided. "M'own cock liked to wander in its day, and, shit, *I* was even took by that'un's looks." Then the old-timer's tone changed, as if he were tired of gossip. "Well, 'tis gettin' late, Slocum. I'd best be sashayin'. M'bunk, it's waitin' in the bunkhouse."

"One more thing, Wasatch—just out of curiosity. Today,

did you happen to notice anybody on the spread—anybody at all—trying to walk around on a damaged bootheel?"

"Can't say as I did, Slocum. O' course, most of the boys has got more'n one pair of boots, would likely change rather than walk crooked, lame hisself. Say, Kyle Reeve, he'll be rollin' in later tonight, fetchin' the boss lady's body. As ranch foreman he keeps up on the boys' clothes, equipment, and such. Whatever'd make their work go bad."

"Er, I don't think I care to ask Reeve."

"Wal, in that case, Slocum—" A pause while Wasatch spat again. "I reckon I could nose around some come mornin'. Tell you what I find."

"I wouldn't ask you to bother—"

" 'Tain't no bother, Slocum! None! I be a snoopy old fella."

"I bet you are, Wasatch. Well, sleep good. Be seeing you."

Slocum listened to the old man's footfalls fade. Whether he'd wanted to or not, he'd learned plenty from the talkative geezer. So Kyle Reeve, at one time, might have been carrying on with Fiona? But that affair had been shunted to a sidetrack, when a new love—Manuel Ramirez—came highballing the main line?

And then Ramirez, a man in his prime, had died.

An accident?

A killing? More than likely, thought Slocum.

But if a killing, then by whom?

Were animosities ladled up from the past involved in today's deed—the killing of Fiona?

Well, he, Slocum, would be riding out in the morning. This killing was the law's affair, not his . . .

"Slocum?" The voice, hushed and grating, came from behind him.

"Back again, Wasatch? Something more to say?" But even as he turned, Slocum felt his nape hairs curl. Something was wrong. Very wrong . . .

A form, larger than his own, crowded close. Hot, foul breath fanned Slocum's nostrils. The other man's face, buried in shadows, was no more than a pale blur. Slocum's instinct told him to watch out for an arm move, and he started to twist in time to avoid the knife blade's stroke—almost. A sharp pain raked down his side. He was cut, probably only slightly: The pain wasn't very bad. His groping hand grabbed the knife-wielder's wrist, and together the pair slammed into the fence.

Slocum wasn't about to raise an outcry. This was enemy country, and to do so might bring more enemies down. It was useless to try for his Colt—his arm was pinned. And damn it! he thought. That's my gun hand! The assailant loosed his arm grip and tried a grab for Slocum's throat.

Slocum, desperate, took advantage of the slip.

His left hand chopped backward and down, and his right stretched out to seize the would-be knifer.

The man was strong—very strong. Slocum tried to put him away, sledging a fist into his side, but the man squirmed to break his grip. Slocum barged forward, on guard against the blade, but in the dark he clutched empty air. A split second later, a knife swished past his ear, and at the same time an elbow drove into his chest. The wind knocked from his lungs, he went to his knees.

The foe launched a savage kick, his boot toe brushing Slocum's shoulder. As Slocum fell back, the other man dropped atop him.

Slocum grabbed his attacker's knife arm, and the two men grappled. The assailant pumped a knee, trying for Slocum's groin, but Slocum, anticipating, rolled aside. The knee impacted his thigh, the pain lancing so badly that his eyes misted. Yet he managed to roll over, flipping the other man. Pinning him, Slocum reached for his neck, but found his jaw. This he pushed hard, forcing the man's head to one side.

Grunting and sweating, the assailant uncoiled his legs

and powered both booted feet to Slocum's chest. Slocum flew backward, still gripping the man's knife hand. There was a metallic *clank,* a rasping low cry.

"Ow!"

Had the knife been shaken loose?

Slocum's momentum carried him till his rump again slammed the earth.

Somewhere on the dark ground, that dropped knife lay up for grabs—but how to get it? The opponent was regaining his feet. Slocum bounded up as well, and soon the battlers were circling each other in the almost pitch blackness.

Slocum shot a blow, aimed at the other's nose. The other dodged, dancing toward Slocum. The long arms of the man had the reach, but he was clumsy, his reflexes off. For each hit he sustained, Slocum retaliated: wading in, raining blows, forcing his foe's guard down. Slocum's knuckles slammed a hard abdomen, but at the same time his own cheek took a swipe. *Son of a bitch!*

So far the fight in the night had created little noise, and no other men came running. The combatants were stalking silhouettes by starlight. But Slocum had no doubt that his foe knew him, had it in for him.

But who? Slocum had no clue.

Now he cocked his right arm and slugged with it. The hit connected, flung the other's head back. He staggered and nearly went down again. Hurling rights and lefts, overhand and underhand, Slocum drove the man—until his back was against the fence.

The unknown enemy kicked the dropped knife; there was the harsh click of blade against stone. Both men dropped to their knees, diving for the weapon. Slocum hurled himself at the other man, landed on him, and the opponents rolled. Slocum's foe came up with the knife, but Slocum grabbed his free hand—and twisted hard.

The foe slashed, slicing Slocum's sleeve, but Slocum relentlessly pried back the man's index finger. The barely

seen enemy groaned in pain, until there was a snapping
sound in the night, a crisp *pop!*

As the finger broke, the man yelped. And then he was
running, his footfalls fading, to become lost like Wasatch's.

It was so dark that pursuit was pointless—and that fact
hurt. Still, Slocum wore a wolfish grin. He'd managed to
survive—again. Sucking in a breath, he let his eyes close,
steadying himself. Legs that had ached from the day's hike
still ached, and the rest of him now hurt, too: head, arms,
and that knife cut along his rib cage.

Silence cloaked the deserted ranch yard. The assailant,
when he'd fled, had taken his knife along. Slocum eased
the six-gun back where it rode, in its holster. He decided
to do what he'd come to that spot for—collect his bedroll
from the shed, then go off and spread it. Off in the hills
behind the ranch buildings, hidden and safe.

Maybe, come morning, he'd look around the spread, be
able to find a jasper with a swollen, broken finger.

Then he'd take St. James at his promise, accept his
gift horse.

And it damn well better be one worth his hanging around
for.

6

Slocum awoke to a bird twittering on the branch of the jackpine under which he'd spread his bedroll. He sat up and reached his hand for his holstered Colt. As was his habit when sleeping outdoors, he'd laid the weapon on a flat rock, and now he proceeded to check it.

It was free of dampness, all good.

Next the big man tugged his shirt open and inspected the slight knife cut in his side. He found it no worse than it had been last night, when by light of a lucifer he'd examined it as best he could. Some blood had flowed, but the wound was little more than a deep scratch. The man who'd tried to kill him had failed even to inflict much damage.

Slocum tugged on his boots and then uncoiled his legs, rising amid the hillside boulder cluster where he'd slept soundly and well. He was a hundred yards or so above the ranch buildings. The day was bright and sunny, a good one to be jogging an easy southbound trail.

Slocum jammed on his hat, just as a meadowlark flapped off into the blue. He was hungry again. He reckoned there'd be biscuits, coffee, and maybe more in the Diamond 7 cookshack. He decided to go down, have a mugful and a bite, then look around a bit for a battered-faced jasper sporting a broken finger.

If he found the man, he'd inquire: "Why go for Slocum? Who put you up to it?" If he got no answers, it would be time to move on, confront Cecil St. James.

Slocum could understand why the aristocrat might want him dead. Loose lips in Antelope Creek could send a sheriff to the ranch house door. St. James wouldn't be aware of Slocum's lack of fondness for tin stars—or judges, or systems of law. They hadn't been part of his upbringing. He was a good ol' handle-your-grudge-your-own-self bird, a unique breed bred in Calhoun County, Georgia.

He'd carried the country boy's way through a good many wars, feuds, and the like. Even outlaws' falling-outs.

Slocum's only problem with St. James siccing the assassin on him was that when he'd left the Englishman, the Englishman had been drunk—dead drunk. If Yolanda weren't a loyal servant—and friend—she could have proved a valuable source of information. But Slocum felt she *was* intensely loyal to her boss and lover.

Slocum wouldn't press her.

Slocum was fairly sure the men in the bunkhouse hadn't heard the disturbance. Nobody, including Wasatch, had come running, and Slocum was still inclined to believe the old-timer to be friend, not enemy.

As he rounded the view-blocking boulders and started down, Slocum saw the buckboard standing in the middle of the yard. So Fiona's corpse had been brought home for burial. Reeve and the hands he'd taken along must have worked all night.

He stalked past the dust-caked flatbed, heading for the water trough, wanting to douse his face with a wake-up splash. But a call reached him: "Señor, will you come, *por favor*?" Yolanda Ramirez stood on the veranda, beckoning.

What the hell? Why not?

"Sure, Mrs. Ramirez," he said, hiking up. "How's Cecil doing this fine day?"

"Not so good, Señor Slocum. He has the headache, *muy malo*. He is liking his strong drink too much. But he's awake, and wanting words with you."

Slocum mounted the front veranda steps, his boot soles clumping. Yolanda held the door, and he walked into the house. One pace inside the entrance hall, he was assaulted by the smell, overpowering, of banks of cut flowers—mostly roses, a few geraniums—that had been brought in, despite the early hour. The gardeners must have been rousted and sent out early—unless female house servants had been assigned to do picking.

"Burial in a few hours," the housekeeper said, going into the parlor, Slocum at her heels. He saw that the divans had been shoved aside to make room for a crepe-decked coffin of pine. The heavy coffin rested across a pair of sawhorses.

A coffin so soon? Was one being kept around the ranch, just in case, at the time of Fiona's death? Mighty convenient! Then Slocum recalled that during supper last evening, he'd heard some hammering. A tool-handy ranch hand must have been working, and here was the result.

There was only one mourner in the room—if you could call him that. Kyle Reeve looked the most presentable Slocum had seen him—shaved, scrubbed, and wearing a string tie and a clean, pressed shirt. The foreman sat opposite the painting of the young Fiona, now flanked with sprays of flowers.

"Morning, Reeve," Slocum said solemnly. "See you fetched Mrs. St. James back here."

The foreman started up from his wing chair beside the bier. "And why wouldn't I fetch her back? Think I'd steal her? Steal Fiona?" His eyes looked like piss holes in snow, but then, he'd been up all night.

Yolanda spoke. "Señor St. James, he is waiting in the kitchen."

"Excuse me—" Slocum started to edge past Reeve. The pine box's top had been thrown back, and Slocum glanced in. There Fiona lay, cleansed, flaming hair combed, but waxy-faced. Someone had closed the empty, filmed eyes Slocum remembered, but she still looked far from good. People—female servants?—had laid her out in a black, high-necked dress. A dress that suited this occasion, although Slocum couldn't imagine her wearing it in life.

Well, one *might* say the deceased looked at rest—if one had a good imagination.

"Wait, Slocum, goddamn you!"

Slocum, at the head of the coffin, froze. Yolanda froze in the hallway leading to the kitchen. "*Por favor,* Señor Reeve! Out of respect for the dead—"

"This son of a bitch, he's got no respect for nothing! All he is is asshole-deep in nervy gall, comin' to this spread! What you figure was in it for you, Slocum? Oh yeah, I heard you asked for a horse—but there's gotta be more than that. You killed her, didn't you? What happened, you chase her down to maybe rob Fiona, rape her? And she fought back, ain't that what happened?"

"Get hold of yourself, man," said Slocum. "You're not thinking straight."

The foreman stood toe-to-toe with Slocum, fists tight. No broken finger to be seen. "Yeah, you must've had wicked notions! She was an attractive woman! Any man—"

"Use your head, Reeve. Mrs. St. James was shot by a rifle, fired from a ways off. No powder burns on her. Then, too, footprints showed us standing side by side. When you picked her up, didn't you notice? Some of the hands must've. Another thing: If I did her in, I'd be a damned fool to hike over here, announce her death, and call attention to myself. I've no hankering to get mixed up with sheriffs and murder charges."

"You just mentioned hiking. You needed a bronc, having killed your last one accidental-like."

"Oh, I could've hiked into town. Antelope Creek's not that far from Breadloaf Bluff. Plus the town's to the south, the direction I was heading."

"So you say. That might be a lie."

Slocum clenched his fist and drew it back. Patience was one thing, taking insults another. But suddenly Yolanda was between them, distraught eyes flashing from one man to the other. "Señores! *Por favor!*"

Slocum gritted his teeth. "Do the woman a favor, Reeve. Button this! Sure, you cared a lot for Fiona St. James—"

"Cared for her! Who told you that? You bastard, I'll punch you into the floor—"

"Kyle! Slocum!" The booming voice shouting from the archway caused both men to freeze. They backed off from each other, their gazes drawn across the coffin to Cecil St. James.

Who looked almost as ghastly as his wife's corpse.

Christ, thought Slocum, what brandy can do to a man. Or is he a dope fiend, too? By this time, on this ranch, anything seemed possible.

St. James came shuffling across the Brussels carpet, a delicate finger and thumb smoothing his limp mustache. His tousled hair looked more gray-streaked in the morning light. One hand scratched his chest through his Shetland lounging robe. "All this shouting in here, with a chap's head splitting! Give it a rest, blokes, what?"

His instep caught a sawhorse leg, and he veered into the coffin. Slocum grabbed it by the edge, prevented its toppling. "Reeve, you want to catch that sawhorse, straighten it? Yeah, like that." The bier arrangement preserved, Yolanda showed relief. She moved to straighten her former mistress's head on the silk pillow, right an upset flower vase. But although she busied herself, she kept one eye on Cecil.

Not that he was going anyplace: The Englishman dropped his bulk into a rocking chair. "A close call that, gents. Gad, what's come over me? Good thing you happened to be here, Slocum. Er . . . why *is* that, by the way?"

"You sent for me, St. James."

St. James looked at Yolanda, who gave a nod. "Er . . . quite right. I shall have my head cleared in a moment—Yolanda, bring me a drink. Whiskey'll do, the twelve-year-old, if you please."

After knocking back half a potent tumblerful, the Englishman said, "Kyle, you'll excuse us? I'm taking Slocum to my office for a few words. Something about the smell in this room. Sod it! My stomach's upset!"

Reeve said nothing, just stood there like an insolent schoolboy. Slocum trailed the aristocrat down the hall that led to the back of the mansion, but almost immediately he was ushered into a small room paneled in cherrywood. Slocum glanced through a window flanked by velvet draperies and looked out on a rose garden, the likely source of the flowers in the next room.

St. James was talking. "When I woke up this morning, they had things arranged. Yolanda, Lupe, Alma, Alicia—all the maids got together. Seems they loved their mistress. They'd cleaned her up, laid her out. Astounding, Slocum! Astounding!"

"Reeve and the ranch hands drove in—?"

"A couple hours before dawn. Or so I'm told. At the time, I was dead to the world—Oops! Bad choice of words. But, Slocum, lest you think Fiona's death doesn't affect me, let me correct the impression. I thought a lot of her. Really, I did."

"Her or her money?"

"Well, of course, her inheritance paid for this ranch, which I dug right into, got the hang of running. To give myself due credit, I've learned a lot about markets, management, judging cattle, horses—even men. Graduated cum laude from my own self-improvement course of reading, talked to experienced cattlemen. Did you hear about my latest plan? To import breeding bulls from Scotland, improve the Diamond 7 herd? I'm no longer the coxcomb my father said good riddance to."

"But, St. James, you couldn't be faithful to one woman."

Cecil shrugged. "Slocum, you, or any man, should know how that is."

"When did you learn Mrs. St. James was considering leaving you?"

"Oh, that."

"Yeah, that.

"Believe it or not, Slocum, I didn't know it—not till she was gone. Till after she'd taken the buggy out yesterday morning. Even then I didn't think she'd left for good; I thought she only meant to spend some days in town. She'd done that a bit of late. Spending time with friends in Antelope Springs. Upright citizens. Churchgoers. I met a few."

"*Her* friends, they were, but not *your* friends?"

"Not mine at all, at all. They're hardly a scintillating crowd, at least not to my thinking. I guess I'm still pretty much a snob. 'Ra*ther*,' 'pip-pip,' and all that jolly rot."

Slocum was getting tired—and not from standing on sore feet. He felt the old anger inside, the kind he'd harbored since he'd fought as a Rebel. Against people like Cecil St. James, the self-satisfied, smirking ones who set themselves above others—not because they held money or land, but because they claimed to be aristocrats. Blue bloods. Cecil St. James had no money of his own, except maybe an allowance from dear old Dad. So he'd won a young heiress's hand in wedlock and then fought to gain control of her inheritance.

But she'd chosen to keep the reins in her own hands—doubtless on the advice of lawyers. That much she'd implied to Slocum. She had the power to leave Cecil in the lurch, penniless. Which was an outcome Cecil naturally sought to prevent—or so it looked. The whole St. James affair stank. Slocum had lived long by the law of the gun, but also a firm personal code. One didn't kill a person from hiding—or hire a person killed. Not with greed for motive, not if the victim were one's defenseless spouse.

There was another part to the code: Don't get mixed up in strangers' doings unasked—for the hell of it. Don't be Sir Galahad. Trouble could come to a man at a moment's notice, so why buy into it?

True, in the past Slocum had stumbled into shit—deep shit. That seemed to be life's way. Well, now he'd stumbled into a nasty pile, and since there was nobody to be helped, he figured he'd stumble out again.

"Y'know, St. James," Slocum snapped, "I haven't eaten yet this morning, and I hear my belly rumble. If nobody's asking me to breakfast, I've jerky and parched corn in my saddlebags. But before I leave this house, tell me one thing: Why have Yolanda call me? To view Fiona's corpse? I think not."

St. James scratched his aquiline nose. "Um. Let's see. My memory's bad. Oh, now I recall—I reached a decision about that horse you asked for."

Slocum smiled tightly. "You remember? To me, that's a relief."

"There's an animal I have in mind, a big gray stud. Handsome riding animal, first-rate in every way. Some Arabian blood. I told Kyle Reeve which one, asked him to alert the wranglers. I understand he did that."

Pawing through the papers on a rolltop desk—including documents, ledgers, and a book stamped in leaf, *McCracken's New Treatise on Improving Beef Cattle*—St. James plucked up a scrap of paper. "Here, Slocum. Take this. It's a bill of sale, to prove you really own Blue Flame. Now go to the corral, saddle up, and take your leave. I shan't accompany you; I'm bereaved, y' know? Plus afflicted with this sodding hangover."

"Much obliged, St. James," Slocum said. In the Old South, civility had been returned with civility. Sometimes he reverted to the habit.

"By the way, old chap. You look like hell. Do I see more blood on your shirt than was there yesterday? You should take better care of yourself."

Slocum took this last as a pretty good indication that St. James hadn't ordered last night's knife attack. So he shrugged. "St. James, I draw trouble like manure draws flies. You should see the other jasper, the one I fought in the dark—so dark I couldn't tell who. If you see him, you'll know him like I'll know him, from a bashed face and a busted finger."

When Slocum exited through the parlor, Kyle Reeve had already left. Slocum considered the foreman's having behaved as if distraught.

An act?

Maybe.

Or maybe not. . . .

Outside, Slocum breathed deeply, of air that was fresh and not cloying. Rounding the corner of the big house he almost ran into an old, stooped man and a kid in his teens that he hadn't run into before. Although they wore Levi's and checked shirts—like cowhands—the huaraches on their feet were caked with soil. In fact, the spades and rakes they carried identified them as gardeners.

Their swarthy complexions and Spanish lingo identified them as Mexicans. "*Buenos días,* señor."

"Howdy, fellas. Say, running into you like this, I may as well ask you something. That blacksmith name of Mueller—you happen to have seen him this morning?"

The old one glanced at the young one. "No, señor. Not have seen that one."

"All right, fellas. *Gracias.* Some you win, some you lose, I reckon."

He strode toward the corral, thinking about the horse he'd been promised and the prospect of riding out.

He was feeling better by the minute.

7

The wagon road that Slocum followed south unwound like a pale white ribbon across the rolling brown landscape. He'd left the Diamond 7 an hour ago, and now, looking at a distant treeline and silver glimmer, he knew that before long he'd be needing to cross a river. He tugged his hat brim to shade his eyes and kept riding, his gaze settling between the ears of his mount.

And what a mount it was! No wonder he was getting attached to the big, muscled-up gray. Would it turn out as reliable as his last horse, the roan shot when Fiona got bushwhacked? Everything indicated that it would. Was the stallion as speedy? Another sure bet.

All in all, he was a beauty, this stud turned over to him by St. James. A steel-dust gray with a mane and tail like flax, he was sixteen hands tall, rangy and deep in the chest, possessed of a handsome head. It was the flashy piece of horseflesh the Brit had promised.

He had a nice gait, too; maybe Slocum's luck had finally turned.

The way the big man reckoned, he'd be hitting Antelope Creek by dusk. First he'd stable Blue Flame, order him a rubdown and a bucket of oats. After that Slocum planned on getting bathed and barbered, taking a real cafe meal, then picking a cow town saloon, set to quench his trail thirst.

As for lodging for the night, he'd allow nature take to its course. His own nature, plus that of an appealing glitter gal.

The greater the distance put between him and the Diamond 7, the better Slocum liked it. Before riding out, he'd asked around the place after the blacksmith, Mueller. Although the Mexican gardeners hadn't seen the smith that morning, a few of the punchers had. Slocum had gotten his information from Wasatch, who'd said the smith had saddled up and departed early. Not bothering to draw his pay. When last seen, he'd had his right hand wrapped—in an old, forge-scorched bandanna.

The crusty old-timer had reported, as well, that Mueller apparently had had no trouble with his boots. His spare pair had been found in the bunkhouse, intact.

As for the smith's departure, Wasatch had been puzzled as hell.

Slocum *wasn't* puzzled—the whole thing made sense. The bad blood between him and Mueller had mostly been on the smith's side. A blind bat could have seen the look in Mueller's eye after he'd gone down before Slocum in their first fight. The man had been in one big, seething get-even mood.

Now Slocum's route gently sloped toward the river, between low, tree-crowned hills. The country had been getting prettier and prettier, and would continue so from here on down through the foothills of the Sangre de Cristo Range.

Slocum looked forward to seeing Billy Linn again, getting started in the horse ranch venture. His only goal now was to go easy and let events unfold.

Wonderful thing, the ability to put behind the whole St. James mess.

Not unlike throwing away an old can of dead fishing worms. . . .

A man scrubbed and buffed at the town's one bathhouse, shaved and barber-trimmed, trailing the scent of bay rum—

such was Slocum, striding Antelope Creek's main business street. His meal of rare steak, spuds, and greens had set comfortably, and as he walked, he looked around. The town appeared to be thriving because of its ranch trade, the big spreads in the region contributing, and in turn demanding all kinds of stores.

Most of the structures were respectably sound, built of sawed lumber or adobe, more than a few boasting actual shake roofs. Slocum strolled by the office of the *Antelope Creek Gazette,* then a smaller structure with a conspicuous sign: "SHERIFF'S OFFICE." Squinting in the dusk, he sighted up the line a general store, flanked by the stable where he'd arranged to board Blue Flame. A two-story hotel lay back in the other direction, as did an undertaker's establishment and—farther out—the church he'd ridden past out near the town's edge.

From the pocket of the clean shirt he'd changed to, he extracted one of his fresh supply of long, thin cigars. This form of tobacco had been his first purchase upon hitting town. Striking a lucifer on a handy hitchrail, he dipped his head to light up, then exhaling contentedly, he waded deep dust across the still-busy-at-day's-end street.

The saloon he'd selected was the Ophir, the largest drinking establishment. By the coal-oil lanterns slung from the upper-floor balcony, its facade looked ornate. It sported a new coat of white paint, trimmed in stripes of blue and crimson.

Slocum, the former Johnny Reb, wasn't affected by the display of Union colors. He'd learned to put old lost causes behind, where they belonged. They and related mental baggage that could deter thinking right in the here and now.

A busy place, Slocum opined to himself, shouldering through the batwings. The saloon was thronged, with most of the patrons at the long oak bar. On a small stage to the rear, a piano player sweated and tickled the ivories. The gambling tables came in two shapes—square and round—

and those seated at them were yet another source of din and smoke.

Two aproned bartenders toiled at their craft, while there circulated at least a dozen glitter gals, all pouf-haired, round-hipped, rouged. Some wore rice powder so thick that their real faces were almost lost behind the masks. The women wore similar outfits: low necklines and cinched waists, with skirts slit well up the sides. The gartered legs displayed ranged from plump to pencil-thin. Most, luckily, were in-between and shapely.

Slocum crossed the floor, trodding on fresh sawdust, not yet gummy from tobacco juice. Puffing his cigar, he took his place at the bar, held up a finger, and ordered Forty-Rod.

Around him, the women worked the crowd, some running cowboys out of money, others attaching themselves to older, steady-looking men. The latter likely demanded what they paid for. Slocum's eyes were caught by a blonde with piled hair, slim but with breasts about to burst her outfit. Her skin looked flawless by the light of the coal-oil lamps.

She made her way to him, hooked a heel on the bar rail. "Buy a girl a drink?"

"Thought you'd never ask."

Slocum slapped a coin on the bar, and the aproned man made it vanish. When her drink came, the woman murmured, "Thanks," and sipped slowly. She didn't talk gaily, and she didn't smile; in fact she looked subdued, as if unaccustomed to doing this.

Well, she *was* young, Slocum judged. Maybe twenty, maybe a year less.

He knew the "booze" she'd been given was cold tea, and that she took a cut of what he'd paid. Also, she was available to go upstairs—with him, or any man. What he said was "You been in town long?"

Without looking at him: "Six months, more or less. Reckon I lost count."

"Like the work?"

"Sure. Better than starving."

"You don't talk much for a gal in this work."

She peered at him with a pouting lip thrust out. "Or smile enough, maybe? That what you say? Or that I don't press my hip to your thigh?"

"Hey, the bar dog might be listening—"

"I should care? He ain't the boss. But you're right, he can be a suck-ass tattle." So she pasted on a grin, showing small white teeth. Her natural good looks showing through, she said: "Know what? They call me Roxanne. Ain't it a joke? My real name's Dottie, and I hail from Iowa."

"I'm Slocum, Dottie. John Slocum."

"You don't seem bad, mister. Even kinda nice. Sorry I was grouchy—I'm just down tonight."

As they engaged in chitchat, he looked her up and down. She had eyes the gray of a stormy sea, and the piled hair left her neck and shoulders bare. The bodice of the dress squeezed those generous breasts, so that they were in danger of popping out, giving his eyes a feast.

She noticed where he was looking. "This outfit, it ain't my notion. Ike, the boss, he picks the gals' dresses. Claims *he* knows what men want. Seems to me, they just want a woman."

"More than you want customers?"

"You said it, John Slocum, not me. Want to go upstairs?"

"It's early, Dottie. I really came in here aiming to play some cards—"

She rolled her glass in her small palm, sighed. Her relief was evident. "A gambling man? Figured you for one. Well, John, go pick you a table you like. As for me, I'll keep on making rounds."

"See you, Dottie."

"See you."

He liked her. Liked her too much to force her into anything. Even considering the line of work she was in.

And there were ways of forcing women that hadn't anything to do with muscles.

He found a likely poker table and was welcomed into the game. I lose five dollars, he told himself, and I'm out of it. Out and off to bed.

But Slocum found himself winning at least as many hands as he lost, betting quarters and dimes. The pile of coins in front of him grew. Three hours later, in the low-stakes game, he was ten dollars ahead, so he raked in his latest pot, pushed back his chair, and rose. The storekeeper who'd been sitting in was far from happy, as he scowled above his candy-striped shirt with sleeve garters. But he could easily do without the amount he'd lost. So could the newspaperman wearing the frock coat, and the hard-bitten trail boss in cord ranch pants and vest.

The big man felt slightly sorry for the mild-looking clerk, collarless shirt rumpled, wire-rimmed specs askew. But no man should gamble—for whatever stakes—unless he could afford to. Slocum pocketed his winnings, then strode toward the batwings—but halfway there, up to him stepped Roxanne-Dottie.

"Slocum? John? You ain't leaving the saloon? Not yet?"

"Well, Dottie, as it happens, I was. Maybe find me another watering hole, fresh faces, fresh—"

"Hush! Don't talk loud." She put a finger to his lips.

Some of the drinkers standing around turned heads, but they soon went back to their whiskey or beer mugs. Dottie rushed on: "Slocum, look here. Ike—he's the boss—well, I'm called for t'go to the back room. Sometimes I'm made to dance for a fat banker or rancher—maybe let him spank my ass. Some of those older men can't get it up, nohow. Most times I can stand it, but not tonight. Like I said, I feel sorta down. So, see, I can weasel on Ike's customer, happen somebody else already bought my time. I told Ike *you'd* asked to stay with me, John—for all night. I know I lied, and don't deserve a favor, but—"

"Forget it. Where's your room?"

"Upstairs, in the back. All-nighters get a room with real walls, John, not a crib with hung curtains. I'd take it as a favor—"

"No favor. I'll pay. Well-l-l, maybe a favor. Y'see, Dottie, I like you in that dress. Or maybe I like you, whatever you might wear or not wear."

The piano player had struck up "Buffalo Gals," and the noise in the saloon went up in volume. In the midst of the moving, laughing gang of drinkers, the woman called Dottie flashed Slocum a warm, seductive look.

Her voice took on a husky tone.

"I like you too, John. I swear."

As soon as Dottie lit the small night-table Rochester lamp, Slocum saw that the room she'd brought him to was plain, suited to the trade. There was a scuffed washstand and a tiny, cracked mirror, an iron bed frame with chipped paint, a lumpy mattress that had seen better days.

The big man glanced around to assure himself, then took off his hat and hung it on a rusty hook. Then he stood back and looked at the attractive woman.

All things considered, there were worse places to spend the night . . .

She was rattling on chattily: "John, I wonder if you'd be willing to shed your boots. I know men mostly don't for fancy gals, but I'd be obliged."

"Sure, Dottie, that's what I'll do."

"I'm grateful for your help, John, freeing me from banker Riggs. Why that old sour-breath—"

"Like I said downstairs, Dottie, I'm happy to help. Real happy." It was shaping up as not being the usual whore's lay, which was fine with Slocum, who wasn't in the habit of paying for his pleasure. He was doing something for Dottie that was appreciated—a full about-face from what he'd been involved with lately.

Like that nasty St. James business.

Slocum unbuckled his cross-draw rig, heavy with his Colt, hung the shebang on the closest of the head bedposts. With the woman watching, he drew the six-gun and put it beside the pillow where he meant to lie down. Dottie didn't comment, nor did he, as he sat himself on the bed's edge and tugged off the down-at-the-heels, scuffed boots.

She unbuttoned her dress and wriggled from it, like a snake shedding a too-tight, worn skin. There was nothing under the garment but fishnet stockings, and these, too, she shed. Slocum was pleasantly surprised: Whores seldom wanted to get naked. She really *was* grateful to him.

She'd shaved her pubic triangle, he couldn't help notice. She was quite a woman, an interesting find. . . .

"John, let's get started. You don't need to make me hot." Opening the fly of his pants, she tugged them down, still smiling. "Goodness, but you're large. Somehow I knew you'd be. I can't wait to get you washed!"

Her bare breasts—tipped by large, pink areolas—swayed as she walked to the washstand. While he peeled off shirt and underwear, she poured from the ewer, moistening a cloth. "John, you certainly have a nice build—wide shoulders, a big, hairy chest. But you've been hurt a lot of times. What's this fresh scar here?"

He ran a finger along it, found it scarcely tender. "Had a little fracas last night, on a ranch a ways north. Healing, though. I always do."

"The story of this body dimple? And this one?"

"Old bullet scars," Slocum explained. "In the war I fought for the South, at places like Manassas, Gettysburg. And since I came west, I've kept getting into scrapes—worse than a trail cook's skillet." By now he was as naked as she. "Say, do you really want to wash my privates? I can do it for my own self—"

"Hush. It's part of the service, John—and fun, you'll see. Just lay back on the straw tick, watch . . . and feel . . ."

She crouched in front of him as he leaned back, and put the washcloth to use. She swabbed his testicles, and he squirmed delightedly. His cock stiffened to stand at attention. "Mmmmm," he murmured, as the woman busied herself.

She wasn't ignoring the rigidity of his member, just making no big deal. More and more rapidly her hand moved, though, and the last few swipes at his penis were just plain sensuous. By now it was hard as a carriage bolt, wagging in the breeze and throbbing.

Then, she popped the head into her mouth and laved his tender part with her tongue, imparting a starburst of inflamed sensation. Good at what she did? Decidedly!

Never had Slocum been so sucked!

With deliberate effort, Dottie treated him like royalty.

Her red, moist lips ringing his eager rod, Dottie's fingers toyed with his pulsing scrotal sac. Slocum's brain reeled as he lay, enjoying all—all. Down in his testicles his juices seethed, seeking release, bringing him very nearly to the point of coming.

She continued to slurp and gulp, and his load boiled over. Upward and outward pumped his raging seed, spraying her inner mouth and throat. "Mm! Mmm!" she moaned. The organ Slocum withdrew was as limp as a cooked Italy noodle.

"Jesus, gal—"

"John, say nothing. Just enjoy." Now she was caressing his softened hose, stroking his balls, seeking to instill more action.

"You've done a helluva job—"

"Hush! You've had the first course; now, next, the banquet. If you weren't totally bare-assed, I'd tell you to hold your hat!"

She parked her smooth body beside him on the mattress, Slocum's sore side up, head nudging his handy pistol. Dottie's fist wrapped a cock fully as hard as the Colt's barrel. Slocum reached out and hugged her, inhaling the scent of toilet water.

Not the cheapest brand.

The scent of violets filled his nostrils.

One of his hands ventured to her mons and found it soft as a baby's bottom, but more arousing. She murmured: "Go ahead, John. Use your big thing. I've wanted you ever since downstairs. I just wasn't showing it—silly me."

Her flesh was tantalizing; her thighs clasped his fingers. Slocum kissed the lips of Dottie as they writhed and kissed him back. Then he rolled on top, the shapely legs parting for him.

His shaft moved to feel her heat.

Slocum positioned his knees, dug them in, then plunged.

Dottie wriggled, guiding his entrance, and as he probed her, she arched her spine and gasped. He began to move his loins in swift, gentle rhythm. Her spidering hands played down his back, and his shoulders quivered.

He began to buck, and she following his lead, thrusting up her body to slam his, clearly loving his anchoring in her safe harbor. She squirmed and undulated as shudders racked his frame.

Then deep in her throat rose a keening cry. Dottie was about to come, and then she *did* come. Her first orgasm with Slocum seemed sublime: She wriggled, convulsed, squealed like a mating she-cat.

As for Slocum, he continued driving, in such control that after a minute she climaxed again—shudderingly. Then he scissored between her legs, his manhood throbbing and pumped, his body surging, quaking.

He groaned with relief and rolled off the woman. As he lay on his back panting, he heard Dottie's clear voice: "Ain't we good together, John? Nice, huh?"

"Yeah. Nice."

"Best ever?"

"Yeah. Nice."

He reckoned he'd nap a bit, then try another bout. She wasn't merely nice, he decided, but great. No . . . stupendous was the word.

"Whores get lonely, John," she whispered in his ear. "Thanks for putting a small, sweet crack in that loneliness. Even just for one short night."

"Yeah. . . . Nice."

8

Early the next day, as Slocum stepped from bright morning sunlight into the dimness of the livery stable, he was greeted by the sweet odor of hay mingled with the acrid stench of fresh horse manure.

He could see the horses lined up in the stalls, eating and shitting, but there wasn't a human being in sight—not until he grabbed a three-tined pitchfork from against a stanchion and began rapping on the floor with the hickory handle. At last a wiry, toothless old-timer appeared in the aisle, lantern jaw damp with drooled tobacco juice, the front of his pants stained with another kind of dribble.

"I hear you a-thumpin', mister. Wait'll I get m'britches buttoned. There, I thankee." He peered with rheumy eyes, recognition lighting them. "Say, I know you. You belong with the big gray studhoss."

"C'rect. I come to take him out. Got a long trail to ride."

"Wouldn't be likin' to sell your animule, I s'pose?"

"No."

"Give you a good price. Could find a buyer easy, seein' how young and strong he is, but at the same time gentle."

"What I said was no, and I mean no. Sorry."

"Then I'll let the matter rest. Reckon the cayuse has plumb growed on you, mister. You must've owned him a considerable spell."

"I haven't owned him but a day, matter of fact."

The hostler spat, a disgusting, brown-slick gob. "Ay-uh-*huh*. Long ride ahead, hey? Then lemme lead him out. Your saddle's on the rail there, untouched, and nobody's handled your boot rifle, neither. Kept a good eye on 'em, jes' like you paid me to." When the man talked, his mouth opened and closed like the mouth of a beached mackerel.

Slocum patted Blue Flame's muzzle as he came out of the stall, and the horse nickered a greeting in return. Again Slocum admired the animal's solid haunches, broad chest, long and strong-sinewed legs. He counted out coins for the stallion's keep for a night, threw the blanket across its back, then heaved his saddle up, cinched it trail-tight, and adjusted the latigos.

He checked his Winchester and found that it, as well, was perfectly intact. "Thanks, old-timer."

"Ain't *that* old, mister. Just stomped a bit by life. 'Preciate if you'd call me m'right name, Jethro."

"Thanks, then, Jethro."

He led the gray out the stable door and mounted, then gigged the animal out into the dust-deep, busy street. He headed south along Antelope Creek's main stem, steering clear of buckboards, one-horse shays, ranch wagons pulled by spans of two, four, or more. If a horseman nodded at him, he nodded back.

Not surprisingly, Slocum was in a good mood: He'd had him one hell of a good night, despite the fact that he hadn't spent it resting.

For a long while to come he'd be thinking fondly of Dottie—whose last name was Weston, as she'd confided after their third and next-to-last sex bout. And now as he rode Blue Flame, his pecker and balls still tingled pleasantly, if limply, and a sense of well-being filled his expansive soul.

The thing now's to keep the good times rolling, Slocum, he told himself. Sure, Dottie enjoyed your lovemaking like a squirrel loves nuts, and she's genuine in ways saloon gals ordinarily aren't. But you'd do her no good trying to be her permanent man. And if you tried it, that's what you'd both soon find out.

It was no good letting a gal get under your skin—not if your name was John Slocum. A big part of Slocum was the itch he'd carried around for years, the inner voice telling him to beware of ever settling down. Well, he was resisting it right now, on his way to give raising horses with Billy Linn the best try he could.

All the more reason he couldn't take on a steady woman just now, perhaps not ever.

So, riding past the Ophir, he chose not to glance in the direction of that huge, looming, brightly painted den of iniquity.

The gray between his knees went on trotting, past the whitewashed church with the flower bed out front and the fat, blunt steeple. The building, to Slocum's way of thought, looked about as out of place as any house of worship in any frontier cow town. It smacked of smugness, of hypocrisy, of . . . well, religion.

On this morning of a weekday, nobody was near the place—but Slocum's hunch was that a preacher lurked someplace around, likely counting the coins from last Sunday's plate passing, hatching plans to pad his pockets from next week's collection.

Slocum's wandering thoughts were suddenly cut off: "Hey, you!" came a man's shout. "Yes, you on the big gray horse! Stop, I say! Stop!"

The owner of the voice, a male of thirty or so years, ran into the street. As he jumped in front of the horse, Slocum sized him up: narrow-shouldered, scrawny, but clad like a businessman, black coat and string tie and—strangely enough—pulled down on his forehead a round, black derby. The face was round, too, but pasty, as if its owner spent most of his time indoors.

Choosing not to ride into him, Slocum reined up.

"Nadine," the stranger called to a woman back at the street's edge. "Walk fast, hear, and go fetch the sheriff. Tell him about this man! And his riding Fiona's favorite saddle horse!"

Fiona's horse?

"I will, Joel, I will!" the woman half shrilled. But she stood rooted nevertheless, her large blue eyes wide with excitement.

"*Fiona's* horse?" Slocum said.

"Don't play like you don't know what I'm talking about, mister." The man called Joel had a hard-edged, raspy voice. "You know, same as my wife, Mrs. Macy there, knows it! Now stir your stumps, Nadine! Hurry and bring the law a-running!"

"He's packing a gun, Joel. I could get back, find you dead in the street!"

"He hasn't pulled iron yet, and he's not about to. Not when I show him *this*!" The hand he'd been keeping in his pocket emerged, and in it was clutched a tiny, dangerous derringer. The nickel-plated Ballard Vest Pocket Special caught the rays of the sun and gleamed.

Slocum's hand, going for his Colt, halted. Frankly, the sissy-type had looked somewhat odd, but harmless. And now Slocum was peering down the barrel of the .41-caliber short-barrel.

As with a gun of any size, the dark eye of the barrel looked too much like the portal to hell. "Now hold on, fella—"

"Get off that mount! Now! Nadine, come help me here."

"About going, calling for the law—" She stepped into the street, a slimly built woman of middle height, whose light-brown hair was swept severely into a tight bun. She was wearing a plain dress of pale yellow, which contributed little to her appearance. In Slocum's estimate, her whole outfit—from button shoes to perching leghorn hat faced with faded tricotine—made her look plainer than need be.

Until they'd spotted him riding past, the pair seemed intent on their little stroll downtown. They weren't quite to it yet, however: The busy heart of Antelope Creek was several blocks off, and the street where they stood was mostly free of traffic.

Which just might give Slocum the chance he needed— to turn the tables on this man and woman who wanted to involve him with the law.

Sure, Slocum had an ownership paper for Blue Flame, but weren't lawmen too often quick on the trigger? Like this jasper calling himself Joel Macy?

The woman reached out and grabbed the bridle of the gray. "There, Blue Flame. Steady, boy." The animal didn't shy from her.

"Mister," Slocum said, "we should talk about this. I can explain."

"Explain how you got to be a horse thief?"

"Explain how I'm *not* one."

Joel wagged the gun like a stumpy puppy's tail. "Then how'd you get my wife's cousin's favorite saddle mount? I warn you, talk fast, mister. And keep your hands away from any weapons."

"Mind if I climb down from the bronc?"

"I already ordered you to do that, mister—or else get shot."

Turning to Nadine, Slocum said, "*Did* he order me to, Mrs. Macy?" This, while on the horse's side, out of the couple's sightlines, Slocum toed the animal's fleshy ribs.

"Steady, Blue Flame! Steady!" The horse acted fiddle-footed, then came around with a lurch. Slocum had jabbed him with his left, concealed spur. Joel Macy was bumped by Flame's great bulk. The derby man stumbled back.

Slocum came off the horse with a leap, crashing into Joel, who fell in the street, the little pistol flying from his hand. Slocum, dropping on top of the man, yanked his own big caliber .44 and jammed the muzzle upward into Joel's armpit.

Up the street, several townsmen who'd taken note began walking rapidly toward Slocum and the couple.

"Lady, tell those gents you don't need 'em. Say it's a mistake. Tell 'em your husband's hurt, but I'm helping, and things'll be fine directly."

The woman's strained, less-than-pretty face turned toward him. "But none of it is true!"

"Tell 'em what I said, lady!"

So she told them. Letting go the horse's reins, she opened her small mouth and called: "You men! It's all right! My husband's being helped by Mr.—"

"Cook. Say my name's Cook."

"Helped by Mr. Cook!"

The nearest townsman, an aproned apothecary, stopped a few yards off. "Don't y'all need us to help pick poor Joel up?"

"Don't he need the doc called?"

"*You* tell 'em, Joel," Slocum directed.

"Don't call a doc! Christ! I don't need a doc!" Macy scrambled to his feet, sweat streaming down his face. Concealed from the townsmen by his body was Slocum's cocked pistol.

"Wal, if'n ya say so, Mr. Macy."

"See you tomorrow, Ned. For my usual sideburns trim."

That took care of most of the curiosity-seekers. Only a few school-aged youngsters lingered on the walk, playing mumblety-peg with jackknives and watching slyly.

"Folks, that house just over there. You happen to live in it?"

Nadine nodded.

"I guessed as much. Well, in a minute now, you and your man'll go strolling on back home. Forget about me, the gun-pointing, my horse. On account of, it really *is* my horse. Let the derringer rest where it lays, Macy. I'm only reaching in my pocket for a piece of paper."

He pulled out the bill of sale given by Cecil St. James. "Here, look. Doesn't this show ownership? *My* ownership of the horse known as Blue Flame?"

Two sets of eyes scrutinized the document, then two bewildered faces peered at Slocum. "This document *is* signed by Cecil," Macy acknowledged. "But the horse isn't his to dispose of! Never was!" Joel Macy slapped his knee, and a puff of dust lofted from the cloth. "The horse belonged to my wife's cousin Fiona, like I said!"

The three stood quietly at the edge of the street, the big horse close, constantly switching its tail to fend off flies. Slocum patted Blue Flame's mane as he spoke to Nadine and Joel. "All right, I'll tell more of the story. Sorry to bring bad news, folks, but Fiona St. James is dead. Since day before yesterday. I might've guessed she had relations in Antelope Creek, but I didn't. I take it the bereaved husband hasn't sent word to town yet?"

Nadine's face had gone pale, and her hands on her husband's arm trembled. The shock of the news, Slocum concluded. Her husband wasn't so much shocked as annoyed, doubtless at the thought of the surviving spouse. "From Cecil one can expect such callousness. That low-down sidewinder—"

"Joel!" Nadine piped up.

"Nadine, you know that what I said is true. The Britisher's nothing but a fortune hunter, from the start, not a penny of his own." To Slocum: "According to the document, the new owner of the horse isn't Cook, it's Slocum. As I read this, you're John Slocum?"

"Yeah, that's me." Slocum retrieved the derringer from the ground and slipped it into his saddlebag.

"Slocum, how did Fiona die? She'd been in good health. An accident, then?"

Slocum studied Nadine Macy's crumpled, tear-wet face. "Maybe we'd better get you into shade. Your porch? I'll talk while we amble over there." Then he addressed the question. "Well, no, Mr. and Mrs. Macy, it was no accident, Fiona St. James's death. She was shot from ambush at a place called Breadloaf Bluff. She'd been driving her buggy into Antelope Creek. As it happened, I was standing talking with her, and a shot rang out."

Slocum filled in more details of the killing, described his brief chase after the ambusher. "I got a glimpse of the gunman," he finished, "but not one good enough to let me identify him. He had a horse waiting back in the brush. Being afoot, I just plain couldn't catch him."

Reaching the house, Nadine Macy took hold of the porch-steps railing and steadied herself. The dwelling loomed over the three, Victorian, gingerbread-trimmed, putting them in welcome shade. Slocum tied Blue Flame, then assisted the woman up the steps and through the door Joel opened with a large brass key.

Inside, the furnishings were less luxurious than at the St. James place—by a country mile. If these folks were relations of Fiona's, they were poor relations. The parlor was roomy, but choked with old stuffed chairs, settees, and rockers of indifferent manufacture. Slocum felt uncomfortable simply looking at them.

He guided the woman to the nearest chair, a rocker.

Joel Macy's expression had grown angrier by the minute, wide mouth working, eyes bright as candle flames. "My wife's cousin murdered, and the law not brought in? An outrage! A *damned* outrage!" He slapped a doily-draped tabletop. "And what about a funeral for the deceased, a proper burial? You say, Slocum, Fiona died two days ago?"

"The condition of the body by now—" Nadine Macy sobbed.

"Burial would've been yesterday," Slocum said. "It was to be in the ranch cemetery, right there on the Diamond 7. I reckon it went off without a hitch. That was the morning

I straddled Blue Flame and rode out early. I'm on my way south, see. Was before this mess cropped up and I got sucked in."

Nadine rocked her body to and fro. Joel stood with Slocum, next to the bentwood umbrella stand. "Slocum, tell me more about the horse. Why would Cecil St. James give you Fiona's favorite? From what you say, you needed a mount, but—?"

Slocum's smile was wry. "I was fooled at first, and I'll be the first to own up to it. I thought St. James figured he owed me for trying to catch the gunman, especially since my roan got shot when Fiona did. Maybe I even figured St. James was trying to bribe me to clear out, not cause him trouble. But why *this* horse? Well, if I was to guess now—"

"The scoundrel," Nadine said from her chair. "He simply didn't want the horse around. It would've reminded him of Fiona—the woman who married him when he'd nothing to his name!" She climbed unsteadily to her feet, blue eyes blazing. "So he gave the horse to you, Mr. Slocum! So he'd never need to look at it again! He had nothing to lose, since he didn't own Flame anyway! No more than he does the ranch—" A pause, a pregnant pause. Then: "Wait! Something just occurred to me! Joel, are you thinking what I'm thinking?"

"Wife, I'm thinking there are things we need to do. It's clear why Cecil didn't send word: He was trying to buy time. I don't believe Cecil is named in Fiona's will. Didn't she hint that to you a time or two, honey bunch?"

Nadine nodded, her smooth, pale brow pinched, frowning.

"That leaves *you*, love, as her nearest kin—yes, and her heir! We've got to get hold of that will! It's likely stashed away, someplace on the Diamond 7! In a bureau, in one of Fiona's wardrobe chests—"

As Slocum watched, Nadine was regaining control of herself. "What you say is true, Joel." She put her hand up and adjusted her tightly drawn-back hair. "And that being the case, we should go right out there. To take possession of the will before it gets in the wrong hands—or disappears altogether! I'll get my reticule, while you go hitch the buggy team."

"You'll excuse us, Slocum." The Macys, husband and wife, had started to bustle about. But then Joel steadied down, a look of concern written on his tight, prim mouth. "Wait. I just remembered. St. James has a crew of ranch hands, beholden to him for their wages. On that blackguard's orders, they might try to keep us out."

Slocum was already halfway to the door. "Your problem, not mine, Macy."

"You—you wouldn't consider accompanying us out there, Slocum? Let's face it, you're a man adept at . . . handling situations. You disarmed me without raising a sweat. If you'd be there to back Nadine and me when we talk to Cecil—"

Slocum pushed his hat brim up. "Ordinarily, Macy, my gun's not for hire. Now, if you'll excuse me, I've got an appointment to keep down Socorro way. Something about a horse ranch with my name on the deed."

Slocum grasped the white china knob and edged the door open. Pausing before crossing the threshold, he cast his eyes about, scanning the neighborhood. After years of dodging trouble, he maintained a certain wariness—one as much a part of him as the big Peacemaker strapped to his waist.

The coast looked clear, and he stepped onto the porch.

But at this particular time, outside at the Macy's house, there actually was a danger to confront. A hulking form stepped from concealment behind the horse Blue Flame. The bearlike man thrust out a pistol. Slocum glimpsed the sun's wink on the bright barrel, and his own hand, in quick reflex action, went for his sidearm.

Slocum's hand jerked out the Colt and came up and across with the weapon while, simultaneously, he thumbed the hammer back. It was a practiced move, second nature with him. But this time his foe's gun was already out and pointed. Aware that he wasn't going to get off the first shot, Slocum threw himself into a dive along the porch.

From no more than five yards off—close range—his enemy's gun belched and spat orange fire . . . .

9

Dutch Mueller had gotten to town the preceding day, having half-killed his tan grulla mare, riding her from the Diamond 7. He'd been crazed then—as now—with the fiery pain lancing in his snapped finger. In addition, the smith was furious with all the world, having failed his second attempt at laying low John Slocum.

The first try, prompted by the ranch foreman, had been cut short by boss man St. James, but only after the smith had been knocked down and out by the torn-shirted, limping drifter.

For the second go at Slocum—that night—Mueller had used a Bowie, not his fists. But that try, too, had failed, and in the bargain the smith had sustained his injury. He couldn't stay around the ranch to be hounded out by Slocum, who'd for sure have known his attacker by the crippled digit. So Mueller mounted up and came to Antelope Creek, where for his last dime he'd bought a jug from a rotgut-swilling swamper.

All the rest of yesterday he'd spent in some townsman's carriage barn, first getting drunk to try and kill his pain, then passing out. It was upon coming out this morning, hand *and* head throbbing, that he'd caught sight of the horse by the porch, Blue Flame. Knowing the value of the mount, he sought to steal it and sell it to raise money to pay for treatment by a doc. He now knew his finger wouldn't recover until set. So he'd crept up on the gray stud, but just then Slocum had shown himself.

Slocum, hated son of a bitch. . . .

Now firing left-handed and clumsily, Mueller felt his Smith & Wesson buck. The .45 slug sped to plow the porch rail, at the spot vacated by Slocum a split second before. Struggling with his bandanna bandage, the smith recocked his gun. Through the filthy cloth, the outline of his hand showed, and it was swollen the size of a blown-up hog's bladder.

Triggering again, Mueller again missed, this bullet shattering a parlor window. Slocum, on the porch floor, wormed among scattered shards, his Colt raised. He triggered, and the gun cracked, spat a slug.

The hot lead zinged past Mueller's neck, and the burly man dove for the nearest cover, a tree stump. The smith again felt scared, was sweating: his shirt wet through at neck, waist, armpits. He held his pistol in both hands, including the feeble right, and wincing in pain, he cocked, then let the hammer fall.

Up on the porch, Slocum's hat sailed off.

Mueller heard: "Throw your hogleg down, Dutch! Give up!"

Did he have that right? Slocum not kill-crazy? Bullshit!

And "Bullshit, Slocum!" was what he roared. "Come and get me!"

Slocum shouted: "I'll count to five! Then I'm coming for you!" Slocum had known men rattled by a threat. "One!" he called out. "Two. . . ."

Mueller snapped off a shot, then broke and took to his heels, stout legs pumping. He thought he had a chance to make a clean getaway—at least the other people in the house hadn't bought in and backed Slocum. As he loped up the street, the smith saw toolsheds, cowpens, privies— and yonder an alley leading behind the town saloons, stores, even the hotel.

As he ran—rapidly for his size—his stubbled, bruised face twisted into an ugly mask. In a desperate minute, he'd made it almost to the town center.

Slocum pursued, bootheels thudding.

A brindle mutt trotted along, yapping. When narrowly missed by a kick, it fled harm's way, quick as it could scamper.

Slocum ran all-out, past an outhouse, a sorry vegetable plot, and another privy. He heard a grunt of surprise from the half-moon door-cut and piled on the steam. Sprinting past a clothesline, he thought he was gaining, but Dutch Mueller jerked a flapping bedsheet and brought down the strung rope laden with wet laundry. Slocum was slapped in the face by a dripping union suit, which he flung aside in time to see his quarry run up the alley.

In the alley, boxed trash vied for space with barreled trash, the stink of spilled garbage filling the narrow confines in gaps between the rear doors of business places. As it happened, no people were to be seen. If they'd heard the gunplay, they were staying indoors. Nobody enjoyed the zing of flying bullets.

Even surefooted Slocum slipped more than once, but managed somehow to keep from going down. He was gaining on the fugitive, no doubt of it. From time to time Mueller glanced over a meaty shoulder, eyes lit with fear.

Then the unexpected happened: The smith plunged among shrubs that had survived amid blight. A few scavenger crows flapped and took to their wings. For a few brief seconds Mueller was lost to sight. Slocum raced along in the man's footsteps, branches clawing pockets, sleeves, gunbelt. In his right fist he still carried the drawn Colt. He hauled up on the far side of the brush clump and confronted two alleys now, one veering to either side of the large, looming hotel.

Slocum could do nothing but wait for Mueller to show himself. *If* he would. There were still more buildings up the line, and the smith might have ducked into a recessed doorway.

Slocum wanted Mueller because he'd gone for Slocum at least twice. Slocum wasn't counting the bushwhack of Fiona—he recalled the rifle wielder as not so big a man as the smith. Plus, at the ranch, the smith's bootheel hadn't been bullet-shattered. Of course, it was easy for a man to change footgear. . . .

Now Slocum stood rooted in the sweltering alley, face sheened with sweat and square jaw set. If he guessed wrong and made the wrong play, he could lose the smith—until the next time the bastard shot at him from concealment. Slocum took the opportunity to punch out dead cartridge cases and thumb fresh rounds into his Colt's warm cylinder. He filled all six chambers—to hell today with keeping one clear for safety's sake.

Hefting the weapon, he took a step along the lane leading to the right. Then he took another step. The passage along the hotel's other wall was now out sight, if not out of mind.

He heard a faint scrape of bootsole on earth—only very sharp ears could have done so. But the sound came up the other passage! Slocum spun and darted back—and ran smack-dab into the smith, who was by this time lumbering back this way. He was trying to hightail, but he still fisted the Smith & Wesson.

On colliding with Slocum, he caromed into a building's wall, his hurting and swollen arm flailing. Slocum, recovering lost balance, reeled aside as he saw the jasper's six-gun come up menacingly. He brought his own pistol to bear, as well. . . .

"You don't stand a chance, Mueller! Drop that iron!"

But the smith, hurt and enraged, was seeing Slocum through a pink-mist haze. There was no way he wouldn't kill the man he hated.

The S & W was a good, trusty gun, Mueller told himself. And difficult as it was to use it hurt, now he had the bastard at point-blank range. Opening his mouth, he roared like a bull. Slocum should have died in the dark ranch yard, throat cut ear to ear. But the bastard seemed to have nine lives.

Eight down, one to go.

Dutch Mueller's gun barrel came level, its eye seeking Slocum's chest. As the smith held steady, his right hand fanned the hammer, his enemy as good as dead. But then a harsh pain arrowed up his arm, and the pistol wavered, going off and sending its slug flying high and wide.

A spear of orange flame flashed from Slocum's hand, and something slammed Mueller's chest, flinging him backward.

Had some kid happened to hit him with a rock? Mueller wasn't sure, but it made no difference. He was still getting even with Slocum, killing him. He grinned a coyote-like grimace, even as he felt another jolt, and then another. He could smell gunsmoke, swirling gunsmoke. Had he shot Slocum, then? He couldn't recall.

No, he had it to do now. . . . Right now. . . .

Mueller felt strange. As if afloat in the air . . . mighty strange. Another thing: He couldn't hear; his ears weren't working. He was blinking rapidly now, trying to clear blurred eyes.

And oddly, he was looking up. Up at Slocum. He was on the ground, flat, not knowing how he'd gotten that way. One thing sure, he didn't recall falling. And yet dirt and weeds pressed his sweaty face.

He brought his hand up. Through the haze it seemed to be red—blood red.

And then the red turned black—black as buzzards' wings. Was he dying, then? His mind rioted.

Slocum! Damn you, Slocum!

He was hurtling down a well. . . .

Pitch blackness. . . .
Nothing. . . .

Slocum stood over the sprawled corpse, knowing that
Mueller had asked for it, yet chalking up the killing as
unlucky. There were things he might've asked the smith,
such as: Was someone else behind Mueller's trying to kill
him? Was the smith a paid assassin?

What had Mueller known about Fiona? Cecil? Reeve?
Had the foreman really had an alibi for the time Fiona was
shot? Might not Reeve be involved in the attempts to kill
him, Slocum?

In other words, how closely did Slocum need to watch
his back?

If the gunshots hadn't brought out people, their cessation
did. Townspeople were running, converging in the alley. It
would be only a matter of time till local tin-star law showed
up. There would be the usual questions:

"Is the big fella on the ground dead?"

"Who's the gunny?"

"John Slocum, hey? That *the* John Slocum?"

It would all take time, establishing the killing of Mueller
as self-defense—if self-defense even *could* be established.
The day was shot to hell for any Socorro ride.

"Slocum! What in God's name—?" The first to pound
up was Joel Macy, long face pale, sweat runneling down
his chin cleft. "Why, I know that man on the ground. He's
the Diamond 7 ranch smith, Himmler or Holmer—?"

"Mueller."

"That's it! Mueller!"

Crowding around now were people from all walks: gam-
blers, bartenders, those who worked in stores. There were
punchers off the range, whores off their sweat-soaked pal-
lets. Soon Slocum stood surrounded by dozens of folks.
Their comments were as expected:

"Another killing!"

"Dead'un drilled clean! Slick work!"

A butcher in an apron nodded toward Slocum. "That's the shooter, there. Him with the smokin' hogleg."

"Run, fetch the sheriff, Zack! The gent looks hard—stone hard!"

And at last, the most irritating remark of all: "Hey, ain't that John Slocum?"

Then: "Damnit, 'tis! Fast gun and sidewinder-mean! Put a bullet in the heart of Quick Bob Mundy, over Cheyenne way last June."

Quick Bob, hell, thought Slocum. The outlaw had been Hickock's prey, not Slocum's. And the place, last January, had been Wichita.

Now the crowd milled and closed in, bawling, those in the rear jostling for a better look. Nobody spoke to Slocum; he seemed to have become an object in folks' eyes, not a man. It didn't make sense, but Slocum had seen it before: being discussed as if he weren't there.

Then: "Make way! Make way for the sheriff!" Along a building wall came swaggering a bulky, hard-jawed man, barrel torso squeezed in a vest of oozed calfskin. Adorning the vest was a hammered-brass star.

The lawman marched straight up to Slocum. "I'm Les Van Eaton," he announced. "Sheriff of Antelope County. And you're . . . ?"

"Name's Slocum. John. And in case you're wondering, Sheriff, this was self-defense."

"Any witnesses?"

Slocum shrugged.

"Three bullets, in the chest. Dead center."

From the crowd: "*Dead* center! Ha! Ain't the sheriff a card?"

Slocum looked more closely at the lawman—his badge-pinned vest, slouch hat, and craggy, bulldog face. Slocum told him, "The fella was dangerous. Tried to kill me before—twice. After his last try, I chased him up the alley."

The lawman raised his hat and swabbed his sweaty brow. "Slocum, hey?" he rasped. "Heard tell of you, so this might take a spell. Say, ain't it hot out, though? Jail office is just yonder, reckon that's a good place to talk. Undertaker'll basket this mess and cart it off."

Inside the jailhouse, it was dim and smelly, the only light coming in through a few barred windows. When Van Eaton and Slocum entered, the badge-packer shut the door on those who'd tagged along from the gunplay alley. Groans and curses could be heard through cracks around the door, but these were easily ignored.

The room held a dodger-cluttered desk and a shotgun rack—a *filled* shotgun rack. Several Winchesters stood in a corner, looking oiled and well kept. Three barred cells took up the building's rear, but there was nobody in the lockup—yet.

Van Eaton sat on the desk, smiled sourly, studied Slocum. "Want to tell the story? All of it?"

"Not much more to tell, Sheriff." Slocum hesitated to bring up Fiona St. James. The lawman didn't look too bright, and the incidents surrounding her death were complicated. All Slocum wanted now was to get out of town. "Y'see, that fella—"

"Mueller, of the Diamond 7?"

"Yeah. Out at the ranch was where we first locked horns. The foreman wanted me thrown off, and he gave the job to Mueller. Turns out, I kicked Mueller's ass. After that, I guess, he nursed his grudge—anyhow, night before last, on the spread, he pulled a toadstabber. We fought and I licked him over again. That time his finger got broke."

"I noticed his hand, all swelled like stung by bees."

"Now you know the true story." Pulling out a cigar, Slocum struck a lucifer on a cell bar, lit up.

"So Mueller had a hurt gun hand," Van Eaton recapped. "Seems, then, he wouldn't be likely—"

Slocum broke in: "Sheriff, he could shoot—believe it, he plugged my hat. Then, afterward, he hightailed up the alley. I caught him, and he made his play, but I triggered first."

"Any witnesses?"

An urgent rapping came at the outer door, and it swung open. Slocum saw a familiar face under a curled derby brim: that of Joel Macy. "Time for me to get in on the palaver now, Les." Macy went on: "Sure, I was standing on the stoop with the others—and sure, eavesdropping. But it was a good thing in this case. I overheard that you're looking for witnesses. Well, I'm a witness! I was in the alley, and I saw the whole fracas between Slocum and the big fella."

The lawman and Slocum eyed the newcomer. "That so, Mr. Macy?" Van Eaton said. "Saw it all, did you? Well-l-l, now."

To Slocum, Macy now looked good—damned good. He puffed his Havana and blew smoke, smiling. Those claiming to be witnesses could be handy—especially if they were good liars.

Joel Macy, it seemed, could lie like a rug.

Slocum merely stood back, let the man prevaricate. He thought he knew what Joel's lies in his behalf would cost later.

The terms might almost be worth it.

10

Slocum and Joel walked together from the sheriff's office back toward the house belonging to the Macy couple. Joel rattled on excitedly, with many waves of his wiry, serge-sleeved arms. "Van Eaton seemed satisfied with what I told him, Slocum. So I got you out of trouble easy: just like *that*." Joel snapped his finger. "You were in deep shit, though. Good thing I followed along to the jail, hung around to listen. My vouching for you saved your bacon."

"I'm a lucky man, it does appear," Slocum said.

"You'd have been behind bars this minute, if not for me. You'd have gone on trial for killing poor, innocent Mueller."

They rounded the corner of a neighbor's house and saw the Macy abode. "Maybe you're right," Slocum said. "Maybe not. Mueller tried to steal Blue Flame, remember—then stayed to toss a few shots."

Macy kicked angrily at another mangy stray. The mutt scooted off, whimpering. "That's what I mean, Slocum. Bringing up the studhorse would've dug your grave. Think how fishy it sounds, the story of how you came by the gray. Hell, without me, about now, you'd be cowshit on the sheriff's bootsole. Know it."

Slocum kept to himself while they covered a bit more distance. Then: "Macy, I don't believe you ever mentioned how you earn your living here in Antelope Creek?"

"I work at the bank, Slocum. I'm the establishment's cashier, a desk job with some authority, but not a whole lot. No job for a real man, actually; old banker Riggs just wants an office somebody for wiping his ass. That's why this fortune Nadine has coming, the ranch and all, means so much."

Slocum smiled tightly. "Macy, I can see you want Fiona St. James's property bad. So bad you can damn well taste it."

Macy peered owlishly at the bigger man. "Slocum, my wife was Fiona's cousin—her only living relative, therefore her legitimate heir. Cecil is just the no-good Britisher whom Fiona was unfortunate to get herself hitched up with. The giddy bitch was something of a fool in more ways than one . . ." His bitter words trailed off.

"When Mrs. St. James was alive, you and she didn't hit it off?"

Macy said guardedly, "Let's just say that she was a most difficult, most unpredictable woman. And don't expect me, Slocum, to comment more at this time on her character. Thank you."

"Getting back to her last will and testament," Slocum persisted. "You figure that Cecil, if he finds it and sees the ranch and money's not bequeathed to him—he'll try and cheat your wife?"

"No doubt there! None! If he finds that paper, he'll destroy it, and either forge a substitute benefiting himself, or take a chance on the courts ruling that his wife died without a will. Count on 'em awarding him the lion's share of what she left. Look, Slocum, did St. James report Fiona's shooting to the sheriff? Hell, no—Les Van Eaton never heard a whisper! Another thing: What about quietly burying her on the spread, no friends or relatives invited? And don't forget another thing, Slocum! Cecil St. James tried to bribe you—and succeeded, presenting you with that fine studhorse!" Joel Macy drove his fist into his palm. "I tell you, I've got to find Fiona's will! And, Slocum, you've got to help me!"

Uh-oh, thought Slocum. Here it comes. Then aloud: "Macy, like I told you before, my gun's not—"

"Ordinarily for hire? Your gun isn't *ordinarily* for hire? But these aren't ordinary circumstances, would you say, Slocum? Why, if I'd go traipsing back there to the sheriff, report I've had a memory lapse—"

A resigned sigh. "Macy, just what in blue hell do you think I can do for you?"

"Ride out there to the ranch with me and Nadine. Hold Cecil and the crew at bay, so that my wife and I can make a search for the will. A thorough search."

Slocum snorted. "Hell, the sheriff could do that much. After you told him of Fiona's murder, he said he'd be stopping by the Diamond 7."

Joel Macy wasn't deterred. "I don't doubt Van Eaton will do what he said. But, Slocum, he's not obliged to help *me*. The place, the money, the armed ranch employees—they're all in Cecil's hands at the moment. Van Eaton is a crude bully, but he's also a politician—he won't go up against a man with all that power, accuse him of murdering his own wife. That Cecil had motive—because Fiona meant to divorce him and cut him off without a cent—and the only evidence is your say-so, Slocum. And you're but a drifter, passing through these parts."

"But myself pretty safe from being charged with the killing," Slocum reminded. "The tracks on the bluff prove there was a third person, the rifleman."

Joel Macy shrugged. "So Cecil will get himself off the hook by accusing Dutch Mueller of the ambush, contrive some bullshit motive. Like, the smith was carrying a grudge against the lady boss—that's the kind of story Van Eaton would buy. That and the destruction of the will and—poof! There goes the end of Joel Macy's hopes. And yes—the hopes of his dear, sweet wife, Nadine."

At the mention of her name, Slocum pictured the woman: drably dressed, drably coifed, leading a drab existence as the wife of this glorified pencil-pusher in a cow-town bank. When she'd first gotten wind of a possible inheritance—and the better life it could buy—she'd seemed as eager as her husband to go after it. Yet Slocum doubted the mousy little woman was quite as single-minded as Joel Macy, willing to do *whatever it took* to carve her a slice of luxury pie.

Now Slocum and Macy reached the house yard and started across. Blue Flame, still tied to a porch upright, left off cropping grass and nickered. Slocum patted the horse's sleek hide as he walked past. Macy was still talking with urgency. "Here's what I'm offering to pay you, Slocum. You'll get a hundred dollars now, today, another hundred when we find the document. Once the will is in our hands, Cecil will be out of the picture."

"And if I take a notion to simply make myself scarce? Just fork Blue Flame and ride out without a backward look?"

The man in the derby stopped, drew himself to his whole height of five-foot-six. He put his hands on his waist in the manner of a woman—a determined one. "You couldn't ride fast enough to pull it off, Slocum, not even aboard the stud. It's sixty miles to the territorial border, and Van Eaton's posse would run you down in less than that. If I let it slip that I didn't see a justified shooting—that Mueller wasn't a horse thief—imagine your pickle."

"You'd really do that, Macy? Sic the sheriff on my ass?"

A curt nod from the lean man. "Without a second thought, Slocum. Without a second thought."

There was no use trying to talk Macy out of it. "When do we start?" Slocum asked.

"A buggy and team are standing in my carriage shed."

"Twenty minutes to hitch up?"

"Make it ten," said Joel Macy, his bloodshot eyes gone foxy. "You may as well be of help, getting the team in harness. Many hands make light work, and the sooner we find the will, the sooner you'll be shut of me."

As it happened, they weren't on the road as soon as Joel Macy would have liked. Nadine had packed a carpetbag—equivalent to a range rider's possibles poke—but in addition, she'd laid out a lunch. Slocum watched with some amusement as Joel griped about the loss of time. Still, eating now wasn't such a bad notion, Slocum thought.

They couldn't be sure of the greeting they'd be getting at the Diamond 7, and running on full stomachs was always preferable to running on empty ones.

So, seated at a kitchen table, in a cane-bottomed ladder chair, he spooned warmed-over stew into his mouth from a cracked china plate.

"Good belly-warming grub, Mrs. Macy. And tasty, if I do say so."

"Why, thank you, Mr. Slocum. I appreciate a compliment, the same as most any woman."

She looked pleased, but her husband sat fuming. So as not to stretch the man's patience to outburst, diplomatic Slocum elected to skip his customary after-meal smoke. Instead, he went from kitchen window to kitchen window, glancing out through each in turn. When he saw nothing looking like a would-be ambusher, he carried the woman's bag outside. Meanwhile, her husband belted on a cartridge-looped gunbelt, complete with holstered, well-oiled army-model Remington.

"I believe you picked up my derringer earlier, Slocum?"

"It's in my saddlebag. You'll get it back."

"Well, we're ready to start, then. Hurry up, Nadine. Let's not dawdle."

"I'm hurrying, I'm hurrying."

Macy waved his key. "I'll see to locking the place up."

"Figure all your heirlooms might get stolen, Macy?" Slocum grinned.

"Not having much—it makes what one does own special, friend."

Crossing the yard to the buggy, Slocum counted Macy wrong. For years he'd subscribed to the notion of "easy come, easy go." Slocum aided Nadine onto the sprung carriage seat, her husband having mounted first and taken up the reins and buggy whip. Slocum passed Macy his derringer, then checked Blue Flame's cinches. Then he lightly lifted into the saddle.

They had to wait before entering the street, it being busier than before, and all traffic going in the same direction.

Slocum saw where: the church on the corner. Conveyances from surreys to ranch wagons filled up space out front, as solemn men and women filed up the path into the building. And from inside could be heard a deep, resonant voice, lining out the hymn launched into by the congregation:

"Shall-l-l we gather at the ri-iver?

"The beautiful, the beautifu-ul ri-iver?"

"Folks getting religion of a sudden?" Slocum wondered out loud. "And it not even Sunday?"

Joel Macy sniffed, then answered with contempt. "Parson Phineas Garroway's fool flock of Bible thumpers. Not noted for their brains, I fear. God knows what they're up to this time."

Nadine's hair-bunned head came around. "But we can reasonably guess, can't we, Joel? Didn't you, less than an hour ago, inform the sheriff of my cousin's death? By now word must've gotten around town. This meeting could be about Fiona. She *was* a member of that church, after all."

Joel Macy cocked an eyebrow at Slocum. "Like I said, friend: not noted for brains."

The small party entered the street finally, then headed for the edge of town. One thought rode Slocum's brain like a glued-on peeler aboard a bronc: Macy's done it twice now, but he'd best not call me "friend" again. I'm bound to tell him to put his words where the sun can't shine.

They tooled briskly along the wagon road toward the Diamond 7, keeping ahead of a high, rolling cloud of wheel dust. Macy heartily shooed the team in the traces, the couple swaying atop the hard-sprung buggy seat. Slocum rocked alongside to the gait of Blue Flame, his posture in the saddle an apparently careless slouch.

Actually he wasn't careless: His restless green eyes warily combed the surrounding ridges and sage flats. But he detected nothing out there that he considered threatening.

For Slocum, the ride settled into dull monotony. When his eyes strayed from the distance, he studied the Macys, husband and wife.

He found them an odd couple indeed.

He'd known other women like Nadine, seemingly colorless, seemingly bent to a husband's iron will. But in this particular case there was more to it. Occasionally—just occasionally—there came a pout to Nadine's small mouth, a gleam to her eyes suggestive of spirit striving to be free. And, Slocum decided—after thought—there was not really too much wrong with her figure and face. The severe hairstyle made her look older than she should, and the poorly cut store dress seconded the motion.

As for Joel Macy, Slocum had also seen his type. Thinking back on his war days under Pickett, he recalled a superior in his ill-starred regiment, a Captain Alexander Fisk. Captain Fisk had marched to his own drum, the tempo the officer's all-consuming greed. Sergeant John Slocum, in his command, had followed orders dutifully. And then General Lee had ordered an advance north through Virginia in winter.

On the march, rations had become short. Slocum had made suggestions, always brushed off by Fisk. There was supposed to be money for buying meat cattle the troops could butcher and eat—but farmers who weren't paid only hid their animals. Slocum grew suspicious.

Finally, when the Rebel troops were starving, near exhaustion, the Yankees sprang their trap.

Pinned down by cannon fire for a day and a night, Slocum's company was cut to shreds. But Slocum, although wounded, managed to make it back alone to Corinth the following night. Noticing the white charger in front of Madam Opal's, the noncom nursed his minié ball–pierced arm, waiting in a magnolia grove.

Fisk left the brothel with his tailored uniform unscathed, brass buttons gleaming, draped with gold braid enough to tie the *Dixie Belle* at the Memphis riverfront. But, worse, the officer wasn't alone. On his arm at the threshold was Opal herself, the woman Slocum knew to be a Yankee spy, from information let slip by a young whore he'd known.

Son of a bitch!

Either way it looked, Fisk was guilty: whether for selling Confederate strategy to the Yankees, or for buying ass and flapping loose lips to the madam. But wait! Slocum could see coins change hands—coins of glittering gold. And it was Opal passing the money to the Reb captain.

It was at that point that Slocum drew his Colt dragoon six-shot. . . .

Now, years later in Colorado, en route to the Diamond 7, John Slocum eyed Joel Macy. He couldn't help speculating: Were there Fisks in the cashier's family tree? There was an amazing resemblance—in face, in hair, in crafty thinking. And here Slocum was backing Macy's play—albeit not for the reason Macy supposed. In fact, the snooping around the ranch could uncover Fiona's killer, something Slocum, on further thought, had decided he wouldn't mind doing.

The woman hadn't deserved to be shot down in cold blood.

Also, bringing the two hundred extra dollars he'd earn

to the Socorro spread, Slocum would be helping insure the success of his and Billy Linn's ranching venture.

And last but not least, Slocum was by now plain curious. How would Nadine—if she *did* become rich—end up treating Joel? Treat him to the same fate as Captain Fisk?

Slocum had *not* killed Alexander Fisk; damp gunpowder in his pistol had hung fire and he'd missed his chance. So he'd gone instead and gotten his wound tended. In months to come, though, Fisk had faced courts-martial, for stealing Confederate funds and for gross abuse of rank. Thrown into a foul, dank prison cell, he'd died, in more ways than one the victim of his own greed.

But the South had lost the war anyway.

And during its course, Robert Slocum—John's brother— had lost his life in battle.

As for John—well, in the aftermath he'd come out west, become a wanderer, never quite one to put down roots, always succumbing to the itch to see fresh territory, to take on a new fight against another of the country's sons of bitches.

So that the notion of starting a horse ranch with a friend seemed no more than a long shot. He was determined to give it a damned good try. But now he was riding along in company with Joel and Nadine Macy, wondering what would happen next to the old Reb with a too-long memory.

Eventually the party dropped into the ranch basin they'd sought, but Slocum detected no danger in the sun-mottled brakes. Finally they rounded the last upthrust rock spur and, from the height, looked down on the buildings sprawl: the Diamond 7 layout.

Joel reined in his team, and the couple looked across at Slocum, faces strained. The derby man spoke. "Slocum, I don't expect a welcome."

"Me neither. You sure you want to go on?"

"Oh, but we must," chimed in Nadine. "We can't afford not to play our game—it may be the only chance we'll ever get to raise our station. That's what Joel says. Don't you, Joel?"

"And it's true enough," Macy snapped. "Well, Slocum, let's ride on in. Got your six-gun loaded and ready?"

"I don't hanker much this time for gunplay."

"I see men down by the gate holding rifles. Let's see if they let you have your wish."

11

Slocum didn't think he and his mount, or the Macys and their buggy, had been seen—not against the dark green aspen and jack pine timber backdropping their position. Especially since the armed ranch hands at the gate had to face the afternoon sun. But he decided to move fast, lest conditions change.

"With Mrs. Macy along, let's make this as easy as we can," he told Joel. "My idea's to split up, you two driving your rig on down there slowly."

"And what'll you be doing, Slocum?"

Slocum pointed at a looming ridge line. "Sneaking around to the gate by another way. Hoping to get the drop on the guards, force 'em to let us through and on up to the house. The men, for sure, were set on duty by Cecil St. James, likely because he expects callers he doesn't cotton to. Like Nadine and Joel Macy, maybe."

"Do you think there's risk?"

Slocum grinned crookedly. "Look at it this way, Macy. Just driving out here, you might've had you an accident. At any time and in almost any place, a man can get thrown from a horse that's rattler-spooked. Or maybe a rock slide'll come tumbling and bury him. He could die from a stroke, or Comanches could lift his scalp."

"Comanches haven't raided these parts in years."

"Joel," Nadine put in, "I can guess what Mr. Slocum means. The things he mentioned are decidedly long shots. But risks *always will exist*—"

Macy grumbled, "All right, all right. I see it now, too. We'll do what you suggest, Slocum, 'cause it's the best alternative. I see the bulging cliff shoulder you aim to sneak from, and the scaled-off shale, the fringe of cottonwoods that should let you climb down close. Especially if the guards' eyes are on the carriage."

"I'm counting on that."

"*We're* counting," said Nadine, "on their not shooting at us."

"It's unlikely they'd go that far," Slocum reassured. "What they'll do is try to turn you back. Keep all visitors off the Diamond 7."

"If Cecil weren't pulling something," Macy said, "he wouldn't feel the need."

"You don't think the fella just wants his privacy on account of he's in mourning?"

Macy snorted.

"Well, then." Slocum pulled Blue Flame's head around, backed the horse deeper into the trees, and got ready to give spur. "There are three men stationed at the gate. When you get down there, keep 'em jawing."

Nadine compressed her red lips into a straight line and bobbed her head with its small, unflattering hat. Joel snapped the reins. The team lurched into motion.

Slocum, for his part, trotted his mount through trees, emerging in a few minutes on the far flank of the conical ridge above the gunmen's position. He put the horse to a rough, narrow trail that wound along a rock terrace. Blue Flame's stirrup scraped the sandstone wall, but soon the crowding rock gave way, replaced by a wider pocket carved by nature out of the surrounding cliffs.

Above was the brassy sky, ahead a stretch of dun-brown rock incline. Slocum dismounted and tied the horse to a convenient serviceberry branch. He unbooted his Winchester and tucked it under his arm, then moved on foot down a niche whose floor was a dense tangle of shintangle brush. From this he emerged onto a knobbing outcrop above a rock-strewn meadow, the very flat he recalled crossing to reach the sprawling clutch of sheds, barns, and the main ranch house.

He removed his hat and peered over the edge, to see the Macy couple's buggy rattle up, drawn by the sweating team.

"Halt," shouted a voice, its owner unseen from the spot where Slocum crouched. "What for you comin' to the Diamond 7?"

"To see Cecil St. James," Joel Macy called. "My wife, here, is . . . er, *was* related to the late Mrs. St. James!"

"You got you proof of that, mister?"

"Never mind questionin' 'em on that, Budge," a second ranch guard put in. "I recognize the pair. Ain't you two the Macys from Antelope Creek?"

Sweetly from Nadine: "Indeed we are. Won't you let us through for our visit to poor Cecil?"

"I reckon not, ma'am. Our orders are to—"

"Please? I'm sure Cecil wouldn't refuse to see us. At least, I think I'm sure. Won't you send word, ask him?"

Slocum carefully edged forward up on the outcrop's overhang. Down below a more familiar voice had begun to speak: "You hold 'em here, Budge, while I go and tell Mr. St. James about who's here."

"Right, Kyle. We'll sure hold 'em."

Slocum first heard Kyle Reeve's footsteps moving back from the narrows, then caught sight of the foreman's slim, erect form. When he passed directly below, Slocum dropped catlike onto the path behind him and jabbed the muzzle of his rifle into his backbone. "What the hell—"

"Hold it where you stand, Reeve," Slocum hissed. "It's me, Slocum." Kyle Reeve froze in his tracks, then slowly raised his empty hands to shoulder level. "Now," Slocum went on, "what would you think to letting cordial callers through, giving decent, upright folks like Mr. and Mrs. Macy their chance to express their condolences to the recently bereaved head man of this spread? Or shall I say, head man up until now?"

Reeve looked back over his shoulder, sneering. "Oh, I don't guess this spread's about to pass outa Mr. St. James's hands. Possession, it's nine points of the law—or was last time I heard."

"Just the same, tell your sidekicks to drop their shooting irons, then stand aside and let the buggy through. Meantime, you and me will just hike behind 'em on down to the house."

"Mr. St. James, he don't like—"

Slocum jabbed him hard with the Winchester's muzzle. "Don't talk to me now, Reeve. Talk to your men!"

Reeve shouted for his men to drop their guns. A minute later the Macys' rig was again churning dust, this time across the yard and down to the big, gabled ranch house.

"I suppose that for hospitality's sake I should be saying heigh-ho, old chap, welcome back, and all that sort of rot. But the truth is, Slocum, I'm sorry to see you here again, returned to the Diamond 7 under these unpleasant circumstances." So said Cecil St. James, as he set his whiskey tumbler on an end table in his parlor. "Feeling the need to pull a gun on my foreman? A rather bad show—"

"Your foreman and those guards you ordered posted, they'd never have let me through the gate in a month of Sundays. Leastwise, not me and these two folks, Mr. and Mrs. Macy."

Joel Macy was at Slocum's side, his compressed mouth a raw, lipless wound. Nadine stood slightly behind, dwarfed by a tall highboy of burled ash, still looking demure and plainer than she needed to. One slender hand admiringly stroked a jacquard chair scarf on a wing-back. The couple stood with backs to the fireplace and Fiona's portrait, in the spot where Fiona had been laid out when Slocum had last been here.

But, of course, the couple couldn't know about the coffin's placement.

"Isn't it true, St. James?" Slocum now queried. "That you stationed those men out there to keep folks off? Now, why would that be, do you suppose? Something to hide, to keep folks from finding?"

"Your returning in company with this pair, Slocum, I'll confess surprises me." The Englishman's hand stroked his high, pink dome. "I sent you off in jolly fashion, riding an excellent specimen of prime horseflesh. You were headed for New Mexico, I thought, happy as a hedgehog in the heather. But now—"

Slocum glanced at Kyle Reeve, over in the corner and looking chagrined. He hadn't been able to meet his boss's gaze since Slocum had gotten the drop on him. If the foreman didn't like Slocum, the reason was clear, but why he disliked the Macys wasn't—at least not to Slocum. What past difficulties had occurred, Slocum supposed might be explained as the mess unfolded.

But never from Reeve's end. "St. James, I want *him* out of here while we do our jawing."

This was agreeable to St. James. "Clear out, Kyle."

"But, boss—"

"Are you deaf? I said, *out!*"

At the door, Reeve said, "If you want me, I'll be on the veranda."

"Jolly good." But as soon as Reeve had shut the door behind him: "The bloody rotter." Then: "One thing that I wish I'd seen, Slocum: my foreman's face when you jumped from that rock shelf and poked your gun in his back. Wonder he didn't wet his pants."

Slocum scowled. "St. James, there's a lady present. Watch your language."

The Englishman laughed. "A lady? Nadine Macy? Slocum, you don't know about this woman's nasty little history?"

The woman's face flushed as pink as the lace handkerchief she clutched. Joel Macy started forward, fists clenched. "St. James, you rotten bastard! Trying to make capital of a dead issue from the past—"

"Hold on! Hold on!" said Slocum, not seeing how getting sidetracked on old feuds would accomplish the purpose of those who'd hired him. Although his curiosity had been aroused as to Nadine's background, he spoke of other matters. "St. James, I'll come straight to the point. These folks are here to see if Fiona, before she got killed, might've stashed a will someplace. In her desk, a closet cubbyhole, maybe a safe."

"That's correct," Joel Macy put in. "So, did she stash anything, Cecil?"

"What do you care?" St. James said. "If she did, it'd be no concern of *yours*."

"It'd concern my wife, her own dear cousin. Damn you, Cecil—"

"No."

"No, it wouldn't concern my wife? Lord, but you've got gall—"

St. James's laugh grated unpleasantly. "No, Joel. What I meant was: Fiona, evidently, did *not* leave a will anywhere on this place."

"You don't claim she left one naming *you* her heir?"

"No, and that's the truth." St. James's hand wandered to preen his waxed mustache. "I'll confess to the fact I've spent time looking. Matter of fact, I've been at it since burying Fiona yesterday. No soap, I'm afraid."

"Any objections if *we* nose around?"

Cecil shrugged. "And if I did object, Macy, what then? A buggering shoot-out? You've brought along a hired gun— one who, it appears, outclasses the common cowboys on *my* side in this affair." St. James wheeled and, with aristocratic bearing intact, strode to the sideboard.

Picking up a decanter, he sloshed whiskey into his glass, then raised it in a mock toast. "Macy. Nadine." He nodded in the direction of the woman. "No, I won't raise an objection to your little search. I only hope your, er, activities won't be an interruption to how I choose to spend my day."

Macy's face wore a self-satisfied smirk, but Slocum thought the man looked relieved to have avoided a showdown. "And how *do* you plan to spend the day, Cecil? Drinking yourself into the state of a spavined chuckwalla? Bedding that hot Mex you call a housekeeper?"

Irritation and more flared in Cecil's eyes, but Slocum put a hand on Macy's arm and stepped between the two men. "No call for swapping insults, gents. You're getting what you want, Macy—why don't you and your wife get to doing what you came for?" Slocum asked St. James, "Mind if they start in the dead woman's bedroom?"

The response was another shrug, Cecil swirling the dregs of whiskey in his glass. At last the Englishman raised his drink to his lips, sipped, then said, "The boudoir? By all means. You've been in the house before, Joel and Nadine, and so don't need my guidance to find your way upstairs." He drew out a heavy gold fob watch and glanced at it. "And now, you'll have to excuse me." St. James showed them his ramrod-straight back and strode from the parlor.

"Only a few more hours of daylight left," Macy observed. "We ought not to waste time. Let's split up, Nadine. You go on up and search Fiona's chiffoniers, closets, and such, whilst I go snooping outside, maybe question a few servants. Slocum, for your part you can—"

Slocum's fingers—busy tugging a cigar from his pocket—stilled. The big man frowned at Macy. "I'm not your fetch-and-carry boy now," he barked, "and I never aim to be. I'm a little too old to start in that line."

Nadine Macy stepped forward. "Yes, of course. Now, Joel," she mildly addressed her husband, "Mr. Slocum came along to get us onto the ranch, help convince Cecil to give us access to the house. And there he's succeeded." Then to Slocum: "Why don't you just smoke, take a stroll, amuse yourself as you please while my husband and I conduct our business?" To Joel again: "Husband, as you said, you'd do well to look around outside, talk to whoever you run into. I'll be upstairs, working fast as I'm able."

Macy glared at Slocum, then stalked out, while the wife shifted her gaze from the big man and spoke in a softer tone. "You'll know where I'll be, then, Mr. Slocum. I'm sure Cecil consented to your having the run of the house and grounds, the same as me and my husband. So make yourself at home."

Slocum thumbnailed a lucifer, lit up his cigar, and exhaled a blue cloud. "I reckon I'll do that, Mrs. Macy."

Without looking up: "Er, you may call me Nadine, Mr. Slocum—as long as you don't overdo it when my husband is near. He's a jealous and strong-willed man, as you must've noticed. And when you add in that quick temper of his—"

"I think I understand pretty well, Mrs. Macy. Nadine. And since we're forgetting the name handles, why not call me John?"

"All right, John. I'll be getting on upstairs now. Be seeing you later."

"Until then, Nadine."

The woman hoisted her skirts and petticoats and glided up the staircase. As soon as she was gone, Slocum started to move from window to window, peering out each of them in turn, but seeing nothing in the yard but ranch hands going about ordinary ranch tasks. A few men wearing chaps swung aboard horses with tool-packed saddlebags, then rode out, apparently assigned to do some fence mending.

Over in one of the small corrals, a couple of wranglers were working raw mustangs.

As Slocum stood watching and smoking, his thoughts ran back to the recent exchange with Nadine. He formerly would have supposed it would be an effort for the quiet, plain-dressed woman to let him call her by her first name, and he didn't know quite what to make of it. Up till this point, it had seemed she was completely under her husband's thumb, but now Slocum detected other attitudes emerging.

Well, she's got that man of hers figured out pretty well, he told himself. I'll hand Nadine that. And if the chance of getting money of her own breaks her from Joel's control, I reckon that's a change for the good.

Slocum deposited an inch of ash in the chimney of a silk-shaded banquet lamp, then strode to the fireplace and looked up at the portrait of Fiona. This time with greater attention than before. Today the picture seemed to overshadow the rest of the room. It showed a lovely young face, delicately featured, yet indicative of the subject's considerable inner strength. The artist had also captured the young Fiona's sensuality, a sensuality Slocum had sensed in the brief time he'd known the woman.

And now Fiona St. James was dead and buried. In the ranch cemetery, wherever that was located.

Isn't it interesting, Slocum thought, that neither Joel nor Nadine so much as asked to see the grave?

Slocum turned from the picture and paced the parlor restlessly, finally crushing the cigar out in a potted palm. Then he strolled down the hallway toward the rear of the mansion. As he passed the doorway to Cecil St. James's office, he glanced in. The Brit, poring over ledgers, didn't look up. Next Slocum peeped into the kitchen and saw Yolanda Ramirez, hands white with flour, engaged with her helper Alicia, making bread. The delicious-smelling mounds of dough were destined for the enormous cookstove, a genuine

Windsor with its oven front trimmed in gleaming nickel.

Things looked normal to Slocum, as normal as could be expected. Returning up the hall, he noticed a narrow door ajar, behind which steep, narrow steps curved upward. Slocum reckoned this was a back stairway meant for servants' use.

Although he didn't feel himself a servant, he did feel curious, and he started stealthily—from force of habit—up. He came out onto a second-story hall, carpeted much like the downstairs rooms. Along the hallway he moved from open doorway to open doorway, glancing into the bedrooms, seeing solid, expensive-looking furniture—of little interest to him at the moment.

Until he came to the room containing Nadine and the prettiest of the housemaids, the honey-skinned Lupe.

The so-called boudoir was a spacious suite consisting of a bedchamber, dressing room, closets, and an adjoining roomy alcove. Through the portal of the latter could be seen a large, permanently installed bathtub.

The rooms were luxurious and frilly, the intimate quarters of a woman of means. The two armchairs were upholstered, one in pale-blue satin, one in pink velvet, and these flanked a dressing table laden with containers, most of glass or tortoiseshell. Slocum reckoned these held perfume, cosmetics, and the like.

Slocum had taken it for granted that the St. James couple hadn't regularly slept together, and the look of the narrow, solid mahogany, four-poster bed supported that notion.

The curtains of the window billowed inward, admitting golden, late-afternoon sunlight that shone on the Macy woman. At the moment she was diligently going through dresser drawers. Tumbled across the embroidered counterpane was an array of clothes, from silk shirtwaists to percale Henrietta wrappers. Lupe stood by until her help was demanded, and when it was, she'd lend a willing hand.

By the lines of concern written on Nadine's brow, Slocum guessed that Fiona's will hadn't yet turned up.

He leaned his rangy frame against the doorjamb and idly watched. Nadine ignored his presence, but Lupe shyly glanced his way from time to time. He found the Mexican girl a delight to behold, what with flashing white teeth, full lips, and her gracefulness of movement when handling Fiona's things.

When on the ranch the first time, Slocum had paid little attention to the maids—there'd been other things on his mind. But now he availed himself. Lupe appeared to be a young girl in the body of a full-blown woman, newly awakened to an awareness of men. She seemed shy— very shy.

Oh, well, thought Slocum. There was little else to do *but* think, as long as the Macys were bent on their search for a will.

Outside, the sky began subtly to change color; soft shadows were inching eastward from the trees high on the rimrock above the ranch buildings.

Then, without warning, harsh noises erupted outside: shouts and the noise of a scuffle. Nadine froze, her hand on a filigree-chased jewelry case. There was a dull *smack,* and Slocum recognized the sound: cold steel impacting flesh.

Lupe dashed to the window, threw the curtains back, and peered out and down. "*Dios mío! No! Juan, mi hermano*— my brother!" The girl's eyes were round as saucers, her hands pressed to her cheeks.

Then Slocum was beside her at the window. Scanning the yard, he saw the trouble: Joel Macy trouble. The man in the derby had the youngest gardener by his shirt collar, and as Slocum watched, he dealt the Mexican kid another wallop.

"Refuse to talk?" Macy's voice drifted up. "Why, you insolent greaser—"

"John," cried Nadine, at Slocum's elbow. "What—"

"I got to get down there! Before that fool husband of yours lets himself in for trouble. Real trouble!"

Then Slocum was out of the boudoir and on the stairs, taking them in racing, headlong leaps.

12

Young Juan, hat in hand, was standing on the dusty patch of ground to the rear of the main ranch house of the Diamond 7. *Madre de dios,* but he was bewildered! The Anglo's barrage of questions had been thrown at him rapid-fire— and, worst of all, in English.

And now the suit-clad thin man with the round hat was angry—very angry.

As angry as Juan had seen a man in all his fifteen years, even back below the Rio Grande, where he'd grown up.

"*No entiendo,* señor. I no understand this 'will' thing that you asking of—"

That was when Joel Macy had stepped close to the Mexican youth, grabbed him by the shirt collar, and with his other hand tugged free his Remington. Macy brought the handgun up and around in a brutal chop, the blued barrel catching Juan's right cheekbone.

Juan staggered backward, off balance, his arms flopping like broken chicken wings. Pain was written on his face, but Macy came after the kid, swinging that gun barrel backhand and forehand, laying more severe blows about his head.

Finally the boy recovered enough to try and defend himself. He threw out a jab that glanced off Macy's shoulder. But Macy waded in again, this time using his bunched left fist and catching Juan below his belt buckle, doubling him over. A looping gun-barrel blow then came to Juan's head, sending him to one knee.

"Damned Mex. Trying to cover up for that wretch, St. James."

Juan found himself on one knee, without any inkling of what had happened, how he had gotten that way. His head hung, and crimson blobs drooled from his mouth and nose. He opened his squeezed-shut eyes, just in time to see a pointed shoe toe speeding toward his face.

Juan managed to crab sidelong and take the kick on his shoulder—just. The power of the blow drove him back; he stumbled on a rock embedded in the earth and fell. There wasn't the least fight in him; yet Macy didn't stop.

Juan was crying out by now, begging in Spanish, as Macy kicked him in the ribs and lower back—the sensitive kidney region. Then Macy bent low and hauled the youth partly upright, his pistol drawn back, ready for a tooth-breaking blow.

"Hold it, Macy! Don't move! Drop the iron!" John Slocum's voice was like a horseshoe file on steel, low and rasping.

"You, Slocum? The man I'm paying to side with me, back my plays?"

"I told you before, Macy, there are kinds of orders I won't take from you—or anybody. And something else: This six-gun I'm holding on you now, it's pointed at your spine."

"You'd shoot?"

"You bet I'd shoot."

Macy wasn't quite ready to lift his head. He released his grip on the kid, but maintained his bent position, waiting. Juan scrambled off a few paces, then darted toward the grape arbor at the mansion's south end. In a matter of seconds he'd disappeared around the corner.

"Yeah, Slocum," Macy went on. "I believe you just might choose to shoot me, at that." He opened his hand, and the

Remington dropped in the grass, not bouncing. "There, I'm no longer holding a gun. I'm going to straighten up now."

"I haven't forgot the derringer," Slocum snapped. "Have *you*?"

Macy had already palmed the ugly little over-under gun, but now he tossed it without a blink. "Listen, Slocum, can we confab? But first, holster your Colt, for God's sake!"

Not particularly set on killing this man, Slocum slipped his Peacemaker to ride loosely into the cross-draw rig. Joel Macy croaked a bitter laugh. "You're a damned odd specimen, Slocum, showing no allegiance to the man who's paying you two hundred dollars for easy work. But that doesn't seem to rub Nadine the wrong way, does it? It looks like it sets fine with my missus—as she stands in yonder upper window."

Slocum turned a bit, glanced up from under his hatbrim.

Macy, awaiting his chance, launched a diving rush at the bigger man.

But Slocum was ready with his fists when the wiry man came at him. His right shoulder rolling, he slammed past Macy's arms to connect to his jaw—just one punch, but enough. The man's punished head was flung back, his eyeballs rolled, and his knees folded like a dropped accordion's bellows.

And then Macy went all the way down.

Nadine, in the yard by now, rushed up. Anxiously she looked down at her husband, then up at Slocum. "You've hurt him badly, John. But thanks for not killing him."

Slocum nodded. "He's out, but he'll come around again soon. You saw what he was doing to that kid?"

"To Lupe's younger brother? Yes. We had a good view from the window up there. *Too* good."

On the wide back porch, Yolanda, the housekeeper, appeared, now wearing a fresh, starched apron. "Supper will be ready soon," she announced, ignoring the unconscious man lying on the ground. "Señor St. James he is inviting you all to eat with him this evening—and if you wish, to spend the night. And you mustn't think it's inconvenient for us here—there are plenty spare bedrooms in this big house. Señor St. James, he ask me to tell to *you* especially, Señor Slocum. Why, I not know."

Nadine called to her: "Much obliged for the hospitality, Yolanda." But the black-haired woman had slipped inside, and the door was shut. So Nadine said to Slocum, "I think it'd be a good idea to stay over, John. Joel and I haven't found the will yet, but we might with more time. And it'd be best if Joel isn't jounced around just now in a rough-riding buggy."

Her husband, trying to sit up, was propped on a lean elbow, feeling his jaw and groaning. Slocum reached down and pulled him to his feet, and then Nadine led him off toward the veranda steps. "John, I'd appreciate it if you'd give our excuses to Cecil. Joel won't be able to eat—at least not for a number of hours. So, I'll just go along up to our room, stay with him."

"Sure, Nadine. Don't you worry, I'll see to all our horses."

Which he did, leading the animals to the big corral, unharnessing the Macy team, neatly piling traces, hames, patent winkers, and the rest. Then he stripped saddle, saddlebags, and blanket from Blue Flame, the big horse nuzzling him, still making friends. Finally he rubbed down all three animals with handfuls of pulled cheat grass and turned them in with the grazing ranch stock.

He hung his saddle rig on a handy fence rail, then drew his Winchester from the boot and tucked it under his arm with his warbag. Then, on feet coming back to normal after his too-long walk, he ambled back to the mansion.

Along the way, Slocum was greeted by some of the ranch hands, who seemed cordial enough—and likely would stay that way until receiving different orders.

Of course, Kyle Reeve happened to be nowhere around just now . . .

Back in the large, elaborately furnished formal dining room of the St. James place, the host was already in his throne-size armchair at the head of the table. The long board was decked out in snowy linen, English china, and genuine silver silverware, plus salvers, napkin rings, bottle casters, and more—all of the same gleaming, expensive metal. Of course, there were two too many places set, due to the absence of the Macy pair. "If it's all the same to you, Slocum," Cecil said, "I prefer we eat without conversation. Joel and Nadine won't be joining us, Yolanda tells me—but then, doubtless you already know. Lupe will take away their place settings now."

Having received the hint as to how things stood—unfriendly, more or less—Slocum stood his rifle and other gear in the corner next to a dish cabinet with etched glass doors. Then he took a seat and bellied up.

The meal, as the host wished it to, came off in silence. A couple of maids—Lupe and Alicia—served, poured, carried off plates in turn as the men finished with them. Lupe, Slocum noticed, seemed less shy around him than previously. She even flashed those inkwell-dark eyes boldly—whenever her employer was carving his meat or drinking imported French wine from his sparkling long-stemmed glass.

Was she being agreeable because Slocum had saved her brother from a beating? If so, he only hoped she had more brothers to save. Lupe was petite in size, but desirably rounded of shoulders, breasts, rump—the important places. Her waist-gathered skirt, as she moved about the table, scarcely hid a delectable set of buttocks.

Turning his attention to immediate concerns, Slocum decided that the *pollo asado*—roast chicken—was tasty, but he'd have preferred a rare steak served plain on a platter, with hot boiled potatoes on the side, washed down with cups of scalding Arbuckle's.

When Cecil St. James pushed back his chair, he produced a pipe, a brier in clipped English bulldog style, with a Weichsel stem and a lid of, again, silver. This he held a match to and puffed alight, then he got to his feet, preparatory to departing. Before he went, Slocum tossed out a question. "You told Yolanda you wanted me to sleep under your roof tonight. Tell me, St. James, you got a reason you don't want me camping out?"

He wrinkled his high, pink brow. "Last time you camped out, it cost me a blacksmith, Slocum."

Trouble was, the statement couldn't be disputed.

Slocum didn't try.

So, alone with his thoughts and a roomful of massive furniture, Slocum strolled to his host's sideboard, on which— he couldn't help but note—stood an inlaid humidor. He helped himself to a long, sweet-smelling Havana, of a kind more expensive than his normal fare. Inspecting the prime smoke at his leisure, he approved, then bit the tip off. When he finally struck a lucifer and lit up, he'd let anticipation run its course and was ready to enjoy.

As he climbed the broad staircase to the bedrooms, he puffed, sighed contentedly, and puffed some more.

Slocum sat on the wide, soft bed in the sleeping room another sloe-eyed maid, Alma, had shown him to. The shaded lamp on the bed table was turned high, and laid out on the counterpane were an assortment of tools from Slocum's small, handy gun-cleaning kit.

The chance to do a thorough job on both Colt and Winchester was too good to pass up.

A man who lived by his guns, Slocum was reluctant to die because of neglected tools of the trade. Although in his thirties, he was old for a shootist and knew he could be living on borrowed time. So now he swung his .44–40

Colt over the bed and, grasping the case-hardened frame, opened the loading gate and used the sliding ejector rod that lay along the barrel.

One by one he punched rounds from the fluted cylinder, then he visually inspected the firing pin and found it clean. Next he used his short, brass barrel brush: deluxe model with India-rubber cone. A swab of soft cotton put finishing touches to the bore—then out came the lubricants. Genuine "Gunoleum" grease for the outer surfaces, "Parafline" special oil (gum-proof) for the action. Expensive stuff at twelve cents for a newfangled tube, but when it came to his firearms, Slocum was no cheapskate.

No dry-fire tests for the big man. Considering wear and tear on Colonel Colt's firing pin, he believed they did more harm than good.

The time having come to reload, Slocum held each cartridge in turn up to the frosted lamp chimney. Turning each one around and around in the light, he'd wipe it free of dust or lint before thumbing it home.

When the five chambers he chose to load were filled, Slocum let the hammer down—for safety—on the empty chamber.

Satisfied, he reholstered the six-gun.

As he stretched his hand out for the Winchester, a faint, quick rapping rattled the door.

Rising, he edged across the floor. "Who's there?"

"Is me, Señor Slocum. Is Lupe."

"What do you want, gal?" But Slocum thought he knew. The young woman functioned in the house as a serving girl, so she was probably bringing him more towels, more blankets, maybe an ewer filled with fresh, clean shaving water.

So he swung the door wide open.

She wore a neat maid's dress, and—yes—over one honeyeyed arm she carried a fluffy towel or two. By lamplight she was more lovely even than Slocum recalled from the dinner table. As a natural beauty, few could hold a candle to her, especially as to breasts. A delightful pair Slocum now saw thrusting proudly, revealed to the nipples by her deeply scoop-necked peasant blouse.

"Fresh towels?" the big man said, accepting them. "Thanks, Lupe. *Gracias*—"

"I bring the towels, Señor, *sí*. But mostly, I come to your bedroom for giving thanks—*muchas gracias*. If not for you, the bad man, he would have beaten Juan still more badly. Now, *mi hermano,* he's laid up in my family's *jacal,* but in a few days again he'll be up and returning to his garden work."

"Glad to hear the good news." He grinned widely— Lordy, but she was an eye's feast. "And like I said, I'm glad to get the towels. Well, good night—"

Her head coming to his shoulder level, she had to tilt her face up to look at his. And Slocum had to look down at Lupe. Her features he liked just fine—the cheeks set high, the lustrous, waist-length hair pulled back to show two shell-like ears. Her sparkling eyes were roofed by dark, dense brows, and crimson lips smiled under her cute, straight nose.

"You're not leaving? Er, you don't want—?"

"I am wanting for give you, Slocum—for saving Juan, but for me, too . . . How to say it? *Chíngame, hombre.*" Her voice went suddenly husky. "Is you, Slocum, I want tonight, and want so bad!" Then, when he didn't immediately respond: "Not to worry, I had men before."

She stood on tiptoe and kissed his lips, and an erection began growing inside his skintight britches. She glanced down, saw, and grinned saucily. "But never with one so *descomunal*—so huge—Lupe, she is thinking!"

His hands went around her waist, spanning it, and he could feel the rapid contractions of her breathing. They kissed again, now with more fire. Then she broke away, and hands moving rapidly in the lamplight, she grasped the folds of her skirt and pulled it high. She wore nothing beneath. Slocum took a long look at her darkly kinked vee hair, while she tossed aside her lower garment, then began undressing him.

He reached behind him and transferred his six-gun and cleaning outfit to the nightstand.

"*Pronto,* Slocum! *Pronto!*" wailed the woman, letting him lift her, then lay her back across the coverlets.

Now his boots were off, as were the jeans she'd peeled from him. "Ah, what a great cornstalk is yours," she said and sighed happily. "Lupe must have it in her! Hurry!"

She threw a smooth, brown leg over his thighs and pressed her crotch to his. Clasping him moistly and warmly, she began to rock her hips.

The swelling of Slocum's cock burgeoned.

Lupe, proud of her efforts, caressed his cylinder of flesh, causing it to swell and swell more. Now it was the hardness and dimensions of an oversize iron stove-lid handle. The woman, wild with excitement, let go his penis briefly and tugged the loose-fitting blouse down from her perfect, silken shoulders.

In the same graceful move, she freed twin light-brown, dark-tipped globes.

"Help me, Slocum," she hissed. "Use these! *Sí!* Use them, use *me!*"

Scrunching herself against Slocum's frame, she pressed his cock to the cleft between her breasts. She held him there in cozy pillow softness, her eyes fixed on his, her lips parted and her pink tongue flicking.

Then slowly, slowly, she grasped his shaft and with his tip began to rub her pebbly areolas, first one and then the other. The woman's nipples swelled to hard, small acorns, the sensation to Slocum a delight, to Lupe—judging from her response—a kind of mad ecstasy.

"Now, Slocum! *Ahora! Chíngame!*

The man reached to the glistening, moist area at Lupe's come-together and grasped his cock with his hand. He quickly positioned himself at the woman's portal, she the whole time groaning and writhing fit to burst.

"Here we go, gal."

"*Que bueno!*" she gasped. "Is good! Is good!"

Slocum answered not with words, but action. Putting strong, splayed fingers under each of her pliant buttocks, he pulled her onto his penis as a cavalryman might don a tight gauntlet.

Lupe stretched her legs high to wrap them around his hips. Slocum was enveloped in the woman's heat, with not an inch more to offer her.

With her groans rasping in her throat, Lupe began to rock. Realizing that she'd spoken truly—that she'd performed the act before—Slocum moved in a harder and harder rhythm. Her quick little gasps, the trembling of her hips told him she was happy—very happy. The big man was in no rush. Looking at Lupe's face, he saw her eyes squeezed shut, her lips curled in a smile.

Slocum was holding himself back, while encouraging the woman's quickened spasming. Lupe wrapped him in her arms and pressed her face to his broad chest, sighing. Her sweat-damp cheek caressed his taut nipple, driving him ever crazier. Slocum, close to climax, lunged, almost pulling from Lupe's depths, but then driving deeply.

Lupe, crescendoing, groaned and thrashed, all four limbs vibrating like strummed fiddle strings. Still Slocum pumped faster. The woman's sobs and gasps showed her on a threshold—but of pleasure or of pain? She was on the brink, that was for sure, and Slocum let go and felt himself build to join her there. Soon her soft, lush body was trembling, her toes curling, internal muscles spasming.

And then Slocum spurted wildly into her depths, hips grinding. Then Lupe, too, began to quake. From the woman's throat flowed a torrent of moans and gasps, which faded into quiet sighs as her convulsive trembling turned to ripples, then stopped.

Finally, she relaxed and lay motionless, as did Slocum.

The contractions holding him within her lessened as her legs let go, and Slocum felt his penis suck loose, to lay limp against the woman's thigh.

Gradually, gradually, the couple felt their strength return. When they shifted their bodies, they did it slowly, totally comfortable, but not sleeping.

"*Bueno,* Slocum. You are *mucho toro.* This thing I want you should know."

"Yeah, it *was* good, wasn't it?"

Then Lupe found Slocum's lips again. The woman's wet tongue probed between them, and as the kiss grew hotter, Slocum's phallus started to tingle again, enlarge. Lupe pulled her face back and smiled.

"Is a long night ahead, Slocum. And who knows what will tomorrow bring? Maybe Señora Macy finds her missing paper. Maybe Señor St. James be mad at you . . . or me, or both of us."

"You know, gal, you got a point—"

"No, Slocum, *you* are one, got the point! The point to make feeling good Lupe!"

And just to please her, Slocum did it to her again.

But the final times that night—much later, and by false-dawn's light—were for his enjoyment, too.

He gave all he had, for both of them.

13

Next morning, Slocum pitched in to a large breakfast of bacon and eggs cooked up with mild red peppers and slabs of fresh, hot bread slathered with butter and plum jam, the whole caboodle washed down by coffee, steaming hot and laced with chicory. When the big man laid aside his fork in the mansion's kitchen, his belly was tight as a Sioux war drum and pleasantly warmed inside.

Which was, he thought, about what it might take to face another morning at the ranch called the Diamond 7.

Neither Joel Macy, Nadine Macy, nor Cecil St. James had put in an appearance yet, so Slocum had eaten all by his lonesome. The food had been set in front of him by Alicia, the Flathead Indian housemaid, and not Lupe. As for the passionate wench dandled by Slocum on his dick all night, she'd thought it best not to be seen with him so early on the morning after.

Just as well.

His cock felt as if it had been drawn through a wringer. And the knife wound in his side, though slight, was mildly stinging him again. But some things couldn't be denied: It had been one thorough-going, ball-busting sex romp.

That was one of last night's accomplishments.

The other was finding out the secret—the one that Lupe had let slip to him. Slocum smiled again now, thinking of it. It was something to keep to himself, maybe use later.

Or maybe not use at all. . . .

In any case, Lupe had slipped off to her housework, afraid of not being able to avoid looking doe-eyed at her man friend. After he was long gone, she'd still need to keep working here. Whether for Cecil St. James or the Macys wasn't clear, though, since it all depended on whether Fiona's will was found, and to whom the ranch was bequeathed.

At this point Slocum was reluctant even to take sides. After young Juan's beating by Joel Macy, who cared if the bank man cashed in on a big inheritance?

Maybe Nadine Macy deserved a better life, but Slocum saw that woman's main trouble was being with her husband. The man was fully as greedy as St. James, but with none of the Brit's gentlemanly charm. Of course, how much charm had Cecil shown lately? Little. Damned little. In Slocum's eyes it had been bad manners on the part of the Englishman, dropping hints that Nadine had a sordid past.

What kind of past? A saloon gal's? A whore's? Slocum had known the like to marry and become respectable as all get-out—in fact, the frontier was chock full of such cases. Had there been a crime in Nadine's background, then?

He might find out someday, if he found himself hanging around long enough.

Slocum shoved back from the table, lit up another of Cecil's excellent cigars, got up, and strolled outside. The morning sun beamed on the showy house and the ranch yard, which Slocum was starting across when he happened to catch sight of Wasatch. The old man was struggling to fill a pail at the windmill trough, getting his sleeves nearly as wet as his brown-stained, tobacco juice–drenched beard.

"Wasatch!"

"Slocum? Heard you was back, and by damn, you be! Heard, too—from that Macy fella—that Dutch Mueller wound up pushin' up daisies, thanks to you and your shootin' iron." He wagged his gray head. "Never shoulda tangled with you, son. After you settled that score, I'm plumb s'prised to see you again."

Towering over the stooped oldster, Slocum grinned. "Had the chance to make some money, and that brought me back this way. Maybe you heard, too, of Nadine and Joel Macy's stake in finding a certain paper scrap?"

Wasatch waved a bluebottle fly away from his blue-veined nose. "Poor Miz St. James's will? Shore, all the hands on the place know about that. So now we're just waitin' on what turns out."

Slocum puffed his cigar, eyes locked skyward on a coasting chicken hawk. "Nice day."

" 'Bout like all the rest. Aches in m'pore feet, pains in m'stove-up back. My advice, Slocum, is don't get old. Oh, by the way—remember you asked me about a boot? A busted one?"

Slocum's interest perked up. "Sure. What can you tell me?"

"Mind takin' a short walk with me, Slocum? I was about to carry water over yonder. Next to the pen where the unbroke mustangs get rode. That's where I'm set up with my li'l old morning's wood-carvin' job."

The pen contained some nice enough broncs, a couple of mousy duns and a blaze-faced chestnut. All three were working on their morning hay allotment. All the geldings looked able to buck fit to bust a man's backside, but the chestnut was something special. The animal was broad in the ribs and heavy in the gaskin, with solid rump and legs for power, and eyes bright with intelligence.

When the men passed the sturdy six-foot fence, the chestnut shied and its hooves shot out, dislodging a rail. "Needs to learn manners," Slocum commented.

"Won't argue with you 'bout that. You're c'rect as hell."

Wasatch perched his age-hunched, bony frame on a battered milking stool and plucked up an opened Barlow knife that showed the signs of long, hard use. Next he placed a sharp wood chisel on one knee, while on the other he balanced a two-feet-by-four-feet, inch-thick cedar slab. Already carved deeply in the wood were the letters of Fiona St. James's first name.

Slocum's raised his eyebrows. The old-timer was working on a headboard for the late boss lady. His gnarled, liver-spotted hands went to work on the beginnings of capital S. The fragrant chiseled chips flew like huge, tan snowflakes, gathering in loose piles on the ground, covering the toes of the carver's scuffed, worn boots.

"You do good carving, old fella."

A jerky, rheumatism-slowed shrug. "Somethin' to keep busy with, more or less. Mr. St. James, he claims he's orderin' a proper headstone for the missus—big and all, carved by a proper stone man from gen-u-ine Vermont marble. Vermont, that's back east somewheres. But damn it, that won't get here for months, and there she lies, in a grave up on the hillside behind the house." He indicated the direction with a vague wave. "Ranch hands carried her there, covered her, set up a bitty little fence. What I aim to do, Slocum, is work this wood'un up directly, put it over her for the meantime-like. Hell, I allus did like the boss lady."

"You mentioned a busted bootheel?"

Wasatch proceeded to carve a T, toiling as he talked. "Just this," he said and snorted. "Kyle Reeve. Seen the ramrod pass the pair of boots, one heel-mangled, to a wrangler name of Harve. For to pay off a bet. And, Harve, *he ain't no friend of Reeve!*"

Slocum caught the old man's dropped wink, but didn't know what to make of it. For a while after the foreman had confronted him over Fiona's open coffin, Slocum had thought the man truly broken up over the woman's murder. Something he wouldn't be, had he committed it himself. And yet, if Reeve's boot had been bullet-punished, he'd seem to have been the killer, and the scene in the St. James parlor must have been an act.

Slocum wasn't much for believing in odd coincidences.

So, never mind that Slocum hadn't recognized Kyle as the one he'd chased on Breadloaf Bluff; never mind that at Fiona's coffin Reeve's grief had seemed authentic. Already Slocum's brain was working on a plan—but he needed more information, maybe a look at that suspicious boot.

"Reeve a suspect? Wasatch, you said before—"

"Forget what I may've flapped m'gums on then! Don't matter beans."

After a minute-long silent session of whittling: "Any more you care to tell me, Wasatch?"

"Like I been hintin' for some time now, Slocum, you'd best to go and ask Harve."

"This Harve. Where can I find him?"

Wasatch cackled gleefully. "Funny you ask. Slocum, that's him, standin' right over yonder!"

The big man followed the coot's finger and spied a man through the stout, unpeeled rails of the horse pen. He hadn't been in there a minute ago. This one's shirt and chaparajos showed hard use—the typical garb of the bronc peeler. And now he was at work, stalking the chestnut, shaking out a supple four-plait-braided lariat.

Slocum hunkered down to watch. Harve built a loop and tossed it suddenly, sent it snaking out to drop expertly over the gelding's neck. The chestnut instantly set about swapping ends, but after several active minutes, it stood head-down again, not even stamping.

So the animal was rope-broken.

What next?

Slocum stayed hunkered down, waiting.

Harve, the peeler, snubbed the chestnut's head to a post, unfolded a blanket, and thrust it to the horse's nose to be smelled. The mustang drew back, eyes round and wild and nostrils snuffling. When the saddle was in place, the cinch drawn tight, the ears went back, glued to the horse's skull. Harve grabbed the bridle, held the reins, put a foot in the stirrup, and swung up.

That was the last easy part for the peeler.

All hell broke loose, and then some.

The big, strong mount under the wrangler tensed, then its hindquarters heaved as the mustang squealed in fright and rage. It jumped straight up, then came down, striking the ground with legs stiff, doing its utmost to unseat the rider. Next the horse reared, lashed out with forehooves, and came down sunfishing, haunches down, tail up. The horse slammed the fence and caromed off, then began to stomp like tandem pile drivers.

The chestnut battled to get its head down between its forelegs, the bit in its mouth between flashing teeth.

Harve hung on, but his hat cartwheeled off and away.

By now the horse was grunting with every kick and twist, still bucking in a circle. But suddenly the chestnut changed moves and reared, to come down with a terrific jolt, almost going to a squat. Slocum noticed that Harve's nose was bleeding, as were his palms. He lost his grip on the reins with those scraped-raw hands, which the next moment let go.

The wrangler went flying over Slocum's head, hitting the dirt in the pen hard and raising a small dust cloud. The bronc bucked off a short distance, then stood with lungs heaving. A few cowhands who'd gathered laughed some, shook their heads. "Aw, Harve," one called. "Too bad."

"Want us to write home to yer ma? Ask she send diapers for to pad her kid's saddle? Haw!"

Slocum, however, was through the fence rails, grabbing the wrangler's shaky arm and hauling him to his feet. "Tough break out there, Harve. One helluva mean bronc."

The peeler's bloody head seemed to be spinning. "Yeah, Thunderbolt, he's mostly outlaw, awright. Say, who th' hell'r *you*? Oh, wait, I know! You're that saddle tramp, Slocum. What—?"

The bronc buster was in his twenties, wiry and freckle-faced, and at the moment plenty bruised. With his hand he wiped his bloody nose and winced, but still eyed Slocum curiously, looked willing to listen. Slocum said, "Reckon your job calls for you to climb back on Thunderbolt?"

"Er, yeah. No way of weaselin' out, I reckon—"

"Look, Harve, you seem a might peaked. Like, if you climb back on that outlaw, you'll be buying yourself a set of broken bones. Think you could use a favor?"

"Well, I purely hate old Thunderbolt."

Slocum drew to full height and began to unbuckle his heavy shell belt with its cross-draw rig. "I figured as much. So, Harve, I'll take your place for the next waltz. Gentle the cayuse, much as can be."

"Christ, mister, I'd be beholden—"

Slocum grinned. "Harve, all I ask is—you remember that for a few minutes."

Borrowing the wrangler's lariat, Slocum walked to the center of the pen, pretending to ignore the frazzle-maned, long-tailed mustang. With a minimum of movement he tossed the loop he'd played—and the bronc was roped. As the big man moved in, the horse tried to bite his thigh. He told it, "Easy, fella. You and me, we're bound for a set-to. But damn it, no teeth."

Then, ignoring the stirrups, he vaulted into the saddle, the mustang taking a step from the snubbing post, then fishtailing. A whirlwind of bucking, back-jarring fury, the mount pounded in a tight ring. Each down-slamming of the four hooves was punishment—brutal punishment.

Slocum raked the animal's flanks with his spurs, infuriating the gelding, sending it into hard, tight jackrabbit bounds. It zigged, it zagged, and it kicked. Around and around the big mount spun, Slocum hanging on, wondering if the payoff would be worth it.

The chestnut reared, almost falling backward, teetering. But then, surprisingly, it came down, as hard as ever, foursquare on stiff legs. But then, another leap, and a twisting in midair, to power downward in a rush, pounding hard and plunging wildly. Each time the horse left the ground, Slocum braced himself, and was glad he'd done so. Naturally, he had broken broncs before, else he'd not have volunteered. Still this outlaw horse was pure hell, new in his experience for fiendish, deadly stomping.

Finally, Slocum sensed the mount tiring. Good. Stuck in the saddle, Slocum simply rode, no longer provoking the horse to extend, enduring the crow-hops and, at last, a wild-eyed run around the pen. On the third pass, the horse stopped and stood in one place, sides heaving.

In a flash Slocum was out of the saddle, stroking the sweating horse's head, talking calming nonsense to the exhausted animal.

The ringing in Slocum's ears started to sound like hurrahs: The dozen watching ranch hands knew expert riding when they saw it. But Slocum felt tired—damned tired.

He left the animal in the pen for someone to tend, and limped over to the gate, where Harve gave him a congratulatory back slap. Other hands followed, grinning and waving, but Slocum called: "Some other time, gents. Me and Harve, we have to talk."

Passing Wasatch, who cradled the headboard, Slocum and Harve sauntered back toward the barn. "Drink of water?" Harve questioned.

"Wouldn't mind."

"C'mon, then. You've earned it, Slocum, for sure."

Harve led the way to the pump, filled the dipper, and extended it to the bigger man. "I purely appreciate what you done, Slocum. That devil bronc would've pounded my balls to mush."

"And Cecil St. James doesn't pay you enough to stand it?"

"Thirty a month and found?" The wrangler spat and joined Slocum in the shade of a cottonwood. Back at the corral Thunderbolt was getting a rubdown from a couple of the hands, and taking it. Here by the pump, Slocum aimed to do some pumping of the man called Harve, who owed him.

Slocum accepted his gunbelt and strapped it around his middle. "Wasatch happened to mention a debt. One you collected this week."

The wrangler's smile turned to a puzzled look. "Why, sure. Nighttimes the bunkhouse gang plays regular at euchre. Small stakes, pissant in fact—and betwixt paydays not even for real cash. Mostly tobacco, hard candy, clothes the fellas might not need. Yesterday the ramrod happened to pay me off with boots. Now, I call the ramrod a damned son of a bitch, and he don't like me—in fact he'd like to fire me for drinkin'. But, hell, here was a chance to get a pair of boots—"

"New boots?"

"Not ezzactly new ones, but not *that* old."

"When you say the ramrod, you're speaking of Reeve?" A nod.

"I'd like to see the right boot of the pair, Harve. The one with the shattered heel. I'd like to—"

Harve interrupted. "T'ain't shattered. I mean the heel. It ain't busted bad at all, only a bitty bit cracked. Hell, I aim to take me a horseshoe nail, fix the thing, soon's I get around to it. And it won't take much."

Slocum pressed. "You're sure?"

"Hell, you're welcome to look. Right here's the bunkhouse. My cot's the one on the end. I'll show you directly."

A minute later Slocum was holding the pair of boots in question. As the young fellow had claimed, the heel of the right one was only slightly split. This was definitely not the bootheel hit by Slocum's slug.

Reeve in the clear, then?

Back to where I started? Slocum asked himself.

In the confines of the bunkhouse, a few waddies sat or lounged on their cots, mending chaps, oiling spurs, braiding hackamores. Slocum looked at them, eyes narrowed. Then, loudly: "Boys, most hired hands don't swap laughs much with foremen or bosses. They ain't often even friends, nor feel beholden to the fellas that badge 'em to get the most work done. So I'm asking you boys: Did Kyle Reeve ride out alone two days ago? The day your boss lady got on the wrong end of a gun?"

"I didn't see him go off by his lonesome, no."

But the first waddy was contradicted: "Didn't see him stay, neither."

But then a tall, rake-thin puncher in a corner chimed in. "Oh, didn't you see him, Bud Blake? Well, I was with him, 'most all day through. Some of us was shaggin' strays outa the brush up along Spruce Knob, and old Kyle, he was on our necks nigh ever' minute. Givin' us hell. And us sweatin' our asses off, chousin' mossy horns!"

Slocum squinted toward the man. "Reeve was where you could see him the whole time? You sure?"

The punchers looked at Slocum as if he'd sprouted two heads. He knew his last question had been uncalled-for. The tall, lean fellow had no reason to lie.

Slocum turned on his heel and walked out of the bunkhouse.

The puzzle hadn't gotten any simpler, then.

Would it ever?

14

Slocum skirted the corner of the barn, heading back for the ranch house after his morning questioning session—and, of course, the bronc ride. But as soon as he came in sight of the rambling structure, a frown pinched his brow, the corners of his mouth turned down.

A horse he'd not seen before—a dust-caked piebald, recently ridden—was tied to the veranda-steps newel post. Slocum had no difficulty in guessing its owner—that was the man standing conversing with Cecil St. James in the ribbon of roof's shade.

The visitor was Les Van Eaton.

The sheriff turned at Slocum's approach. "Well, look who's here. Course it's no surprise, Slocum. Cecil, he told me you were on the spread someplace."

"Over at the bronc-busting pens, to be exact. Wound up taking a morning ride."

St. James's eyes narrowed as he commented, "I'll admit I thought your clothes looked roughed up and dusty, considering the early hour. But more to the point, old chap, Sheriff Les, here, tells me you're not exactly on his list of favorite acquaintances. Something about suspicions that naturally come to mind, you being a rather notorious gun-handling bloke."

"I told you before, Sheriff. I swapped shots with Dutch Mueller in self-defense."

Van Eaton spoke casually, yet icily. "So *you* claim, Slocum, and Joel Macy backed you when we had our confab in town. But I wonder—would he be so willing to back your word today?"

Cecil thrust in: "Slocum, I mentioned your little falling out with Joel. Some servants who witnessed the affray came forward with their version. Noble of you to intercede for an underdog Mexican, and all that rot, but maybe this time you sawed through the limb you've been perched on. And maybe it's about to pitch you into a dung heap."

"Sheriff, isn't it a pity," Slocum said, "that you're forced to get all this news secondhand? Macy hasn't talked with you, true? Nor does he aim to, I'm betting. He's indisposed, as they say—meaning his jaw still hurts where I punched him, and he aims to stay holed up in his guest room. Isn't that the message Joel's wife sent down with the maid?"

There was a short silence, and the lawman's face registered more belligerence. But it was St. James who spoke first. "All of it's regrettable, Slocum. Damned regrettable. The sheriff is going to have to leave without talking to Joel." Then turning to the lawman: "As I was saying before Slocum strolled over, Les: So good of you to stop by, inquire how I'm bearing up under the loss of poor Fiona."

The badge-packer and the aristocrat shook hands warmly, which didn't go far toward making Slocum's day. Joel Macy's words came to mind, to the effect that Van Eaton could be counted on always to take the safest side. And with St. James in possession of the ranch—and presumably all his wife's bequests—the safest side was his side. Now, scarcely glancing at Slocum, Van Eaton moved to his horse, stepped into leather, and swung up.

"Be seeing you again, Cecil. And so long to you, too, Slocum. Get the hint, fella? My considerin' that your best bet'd be to make tracks from this neck of the woods?"

"Don't worry on that score, Sheriff. I'm not in love with it here."

"Then maybe I won't be layin' eyes on you again. I purely hope not!"

He reined the piebald around, put heels to its sides, and trotted off. When he was through the ranch gate, he lifted his mount to a high lope—but out across the range, not along the wagon road.

Cecil St. James sank heavily into the wide seat of a veranda rocker. "Are you wondering, Slocum, why the sheriff's not heading straight for Antelope Creek? Let me satisfy your curiosity. Les—on his way here to pay his condolences—took a swing past Breadloaf Bluff. He means to do it again on his way back, do more reading sign, looking for evidence—the things lawmen do while establishing a murder suspect. What it boils down to, my man, is that *you* may not be off the hook, after all."

"For killing Fiona? That ground's been covered before, St. James. You and I know it makes no sense for me to have done it. One point you *might* clear up for me, though: You and the sheriff, you're close as pickles in a tight barrel?"

The Englishman smiled mirthlessly. "Yes, Les Van Eaton and I call each other friends, Slocum. Lately we've come to think of each other in that light—something in the nature of 'you scratch my back and I'll scratch yours.' You've heard the saying? Now let me ask you something: When will the Macys clear off my property? Any chance you'd use your powers of persuasion?"

Slocum's face darkened. "I don't sell out folks I'm working for."

"Really? How quaint!" St. James's laugh was oddly high-pitched. Due to strain . . . or guilt, maybe? If not for shooting his spouse, then for wrongfully disposing of her will and testament?

Slocum said, "St. James, I'm going now to the room I slept in, get my rifle in order, pack my warbag, and prepare to ride on south. Where I was headed before Fiona got killed. But don't take it that I'm speaking for the Macys.

They'll stop pestering you when they're good and ready."

"Cheers, Slocum." St. James. said. He was still halfheart-edly rocking, twirling his dandified mustache ends. Then, abruptly, he snapped Slocum a military-style salute.

Slocum walked past him into the big, almost silent man-sion. He avoided glancing into the parlor, with its portrait of a dead woman over a dead hearth; instead he moved, cat-quietly, up the main staircase.

In the boudoir that had been Fiona's, Nadine and Lupe were again at it, looking for the will. Some furniture pieces had been moved, cushions stripped from their casings, the rug turned back.

Lupe glanced up, and a knowing twinkle shone in her eye. But it was Nadine who got to her feet, dusted her skirts where she'd been kneeling, and came out in the hallway to talk.

"Morning, Nadine. You haven't found the paper yet?"

"No—and I'm starting to feel afraid I won't. Time's run-ning out. I don't care to spend another hellish night under this roof. And Joel certainly isn't any help at looking." She cast her gaze up at Slocum and lightly flushed. "That was quite a blow you gave him, John. Oh, I'm not saying he didn't have it coming—he did. But today he won't come out of our room, just sits complaining of his sore jaw and a headache. But his face *is* pretty swollen."

"It's easier to beat up gardener kids than grown men. Maybe he learned a lesson."

"Or maybe he's using the incident to fuel his bitterness." A cloud crossed the woman's features. "But that's another story. My problem now is Joel's drinking. He's got a bottle of brandy—innocently brought by Lupe—and is knocking it back fast. At least, he was a few minutes ago. But, John, the reason I stopped you when I saw you passing—?"

"I'm listening, Nadine."

"Just this: You no longer need feel responsible for us. You succeeded at what you were hired for—getting us access to this house. Here, consider yourself all paid up."

She took his hand and slipped him a crumpled bank note. "This will run my household money a bit low, but Joel still has his bank salary, and we can get by." She half-turned, looking downcast. "Oh, John, I had such hopes for a while! The notion I might be an heir—"

"Did your cousin really say she was leaving you her ranch and money?"

"Yes, more than a year ago. She'd gotten pretty well fed up with Cecil, was already thinking of dissolving the marriage. Someone else—a man she'd secretly been in love with—had recently died."

Slocum nodded. The Mexican mentioned by old Wasatch. Manuel Ramirez.

Nadine Macy raised her face, and Slocum caught a faint whiff of perfume. "Anyway," the woman went on, "Fiona told me she'd been thinking more and more of family— and therefore me, her cousin. She told me how important family was—more, even, than the religion she'd started to delve into. I suspect she felt sorry for me."

"Anybody with a husband like yours—"

Nadine glanced at Lupe, saw her busily engaged, then went on talking with her voice lowered. "Oh, John. There was more to pity me for than just Joel. The scandal that brought me out west in the first place—nasty, simply nasty. Perhaps you guessed that from the remark Cecil made. He's nasty, too."

"You don't need to tell me any more, Nadine."

"Frankly, I didn't mean to."

"Keep this greenback," Slocum insisted. "Your husband's first hundred was plenty pay for me. Especially since it bought him a sore jaw."

"So, you'll be riding out?"

"This pard I got lined up down Socorro way—he's expecting me to help start up our horse ranch. I'm overdue getting there. Yeah, I'm figuring to leave later today—aboard Blue

Flame. But I do have a few farewells to say around the Diamond 7."

"The best of luck to you, John Slocum."

"Good luck to you, too, Nadine."

"One other thing. I won't be needing Lupe's help much longer. You'll have a chance to say your tender good-byes."

"You know about us?" *Jesus!*

Lupe was standing behind the Macy woman, turkey-feather duster under one arm, nodding. "Yes, Slocum. Señora Macy, she know. Lupe, she cannot keep her feelings from show."

Slocum ambled down the hall, shaking his head. "Damn," he muttered.

When he passed Joel's room, he heard a groan, accompanied by the musical clink of bottle neck to drinking glass.

Slocum was in his room, with his possibles packet gathered and tied and resting next to his Winchester on the bed.

He stood at the washstand, peering into the mirror, just having decided not to bother shaving before he left.

The knock on the door was faint, but insistent.

"Is me, Slocum. Let in, *por favor.*"

"Lupe?"

"*Sí.* Lupe."

He thought he knew what was on tap, but he opened the door anyway.

And when the panel swung wide, the dusky-skinned woman rushed into his arms, grabbed him around the upper body, and gave him a hard, wet kiss on the mouth. The door swung closed again, thanks to her barefoot kick. Slocum thought again that the nicest thing about the Mexican girl—besides those flashing eyes—was the skein of lustrous hair, black as a grackle's wing. Or was it the hot, moist mouth that now roamed his face, neck, earlobes—enough to bring his erection to bear on his britches front?

"Oh, Slocum, you are going away! *Mañana,* you will be nowhere near Lupe. She is knowing this must be, but wants we enjoy each other again—before she see you no more. *Ahora,* Slocum?"

She held him fast around the arms and waist, her face upturned, her full, crimson lips parted.

"Well, if you reckon there won't any bell-pull get rung, calling you to wait on St. James—"

"Not will be, Slocum! Now is good time, like I saying! *Ahora! Me gusto!*"

Lupe broke from the big man, dragged down her scooped blouse to expose those breasts, and the wide, deep cleavage between. At the same time her hand wormed past his fly buttons, sought and found his by-now railspike-stiff manhood.

When she'd dragged his cock out into the open, she promptly whirled and threw up the folds of her skirt. As before, Slocum saw all she had to show. Now she bent forward from the waist, offering him her bountiful, pale brown backside.

Slocum got an all-encompassing view of buttocks, full thighs, and, at the apex of her vee, strands of kinky black pubic hair. Lupe, flaunting her cheeks, backed toward him. His hands grasped her trembling flanks and spread them.

In the bright window light, her pink nether lips shone as if dewdrop-kissed.

Slocum, aroused past the point of caution, flexed his knees to lower his stance and position his stiff dick for a quick down-angled coupling. "Ah, Slocum, *querido! Chíngame! Chíngame!*"

But just as Slocum's tip met her yearning portal, his ears caught an onslaught of distracting racket. Through the open window came the *clop-clop* of horses' hooves—many horses' hooves. Arrivals were rolling into the yard, harness leather creaking and wagons rumbling.

"Jesus Christ, now what?"

"*Nombre de Dios*," moaned Lupe. "What is it, Slocum? Señor St. James, he is having the visitors?"

Crouching to keep his head low and peep over the windowsill, Slocum conned the outer area. Through the veil of sooty dust he saw them: visitors, right enough— a passel of them! The yard of the Diamond 7 was filling up with teams and vehicles, running the gamut from fringe-top surreys, to buckboards, to ancient, weathered, slat-side wagons.

Most were driven by adult males in plain-cut workmen's garb, but there were plenty of women on the seats, and more than a few kids, both teenaged and younger.

Slocum saw Cecil St. James, his face livid, striding toward the bow-bonneted, deep-bodied Studebaker in the lead. Things seemed serious, for he'd donned his big cream hat. Halfway across the yard he was joined by Kyle Reeve, who fell into step with his long-legged employer.

Back up in the room: "Slocum?" Lupe breathed.

"There's something unpleasant brewing, gal. I can smell it. And the place for me now isn't inside these house walls. I'm going out there."

"To help Señora Macy? Sẽnor St. James?"

"To help myself, mostly, Lupe." He was checking his Colt, then snatching up his rifle. "You stay clear of any gunplay, hear? And if you get a chance, pass the advice to Nadine Macy."

Then he was out of the hall and clattering down the servants' stairs. Halfway down he halted, looked down at himself below the belt, and sighed. He propped the Winchester against the narrow landing's corner. Smiling a bit, he hastily did up the buttons of his fly.

Keep your cock in your pants, Slocum, and your head on your shoulders, he told himself.

And, oh yeah. Keep your hand on your gun, and unlimber your trigger finger.

15

"What the devil do you blighters mean, coming on my land?" The shout of outrage—with a lilting British accent—rolled from the strong lungs of Cecil St. James in the hot morning.

The Englishman planted himself, legs apart and mustachio twitching, in the path of the lead wagon of the arriving cavalcade. The driver of that conveyance—a wiry, chinless individual with a face like a rat—was forced to pull rein. His team and its burden lumbered to a halt, as ranch-yard dust was roiled by the wagon's dragging braked wheels.

The horse-drawn vehicles that followed, their way blocked, rolled to a collective stop, their numbers stretching all the way back to the gate. Slocum, coming down the mansion steps, studied them with interest.

His earliest assessment was correct: Most of the people were sodbuster types from the git-go. The men's hands were stained with soil, and heavily calloused from plow handles. The women were somber-faced and unsmiling, wearing aprons of frayed calico over long-sleeved dresses. Their heads were shielded by faded sunbonnets.

St. James had to be kicking himself now, for disbanding the gate guard and sending his men back about their ranch work. But who could have foreseen the need to keep out pesky arrivals, once Joel Macy and his wife—with Slocum—had barged in yesterday?

Slocum quietly slipped among the ranch hands rallying to their boss, standing in a knot behind him. The cowboys were edgy, letting their hands hover near their six-gun handles. Slocum was relieved to see that none had drawn the weapons—at least not yet.

"Can't you folks in the wagons hear?" St. James's voice sounded even angrier than a moment ago. "I said, what the devil—" But then the rancher's words died, effectively cut off by the man who pushed from under the wagon's bonnet to join the driver.

It had to be admitted: Most folks would think the man imposing. In his long claw-hammer coat of black broad-cloth, he not only looked tall, but was—a few inches taller, even, than John Slocum. And judging from what could be seen above the splashboards—everything above his knees— the fellow was well-built, formidable.

A big, good-looking one, decided Slocum. That is, if you're not put off by the parson look. 'Cause that's sure what those duds do give the fella.

"Phineas Garroway! You? At this ranch?" Cecil St. James seemed taken aback. But his chin still thrust forward aggressively, the muscles along his jawline working like farriers' pincers.

Garroway. Slocum recalled the name. He, St. James, and the hands were looking at the parson of the Antelope Creek church. The one Joel Macy held in not-so-mild contempt.

Slocum studied the man. Besides the distinctive coat of black, he wore a high black hat, white shirt, and string tie. His face was craggy and lined, but he was no older than late middle age, to judge by his dense black spade beard and sidewhiskers. As for his upper lip, it was shaved like his cheeks, while his deep-set pale eyes were remarkably bright, so bright as to look feverish.

He held up a clean, soft finger, as if to end further discussion of his rights. "Greetings, Brother St. James." The voice was deep, resonant, and preacherly.

"Man, don't call me 'brother'!" St. James flared. "I'm not one of your bloody-fool congregation!"

"*Mr.* St. James, then." A pause, then: "Why, you ask, have I journeyed here, Mr. St. James? Why, to come to terms. Sir, we have to talk."

St. James was blustering. "But, why . . . why *them*? His weary arm gesture took in Garroway's flock. "See here, Garroway—"

The bearded man smiled, whiskers bushing. His pale, soft hands fidgeted to smooth his coat lapels. "I call you *Mr.* St. James. The least you can do is call me *Reverend* Garroway!"

The Englishman fumed, but consented. "You want to talk, we'll converse. But don't push me, *Reverend.*" Chin thrust out haughtily, he squinted at his visitor. "How private need the talk be?"

"Not at all private," Garroway retorted. "All my people, here, know what's to be said."

St. James sneered. "I don't. I'm forced to spend time standing, listening."

From under the coat, Garroway drew a long, brown envelope. Slocum saw a wax seal and red ribbon tape.

"You should read this." Parson Garroway waved a paper. "But before you do, let me caution you—Lawyer Bagge, a member of my congregation, testifies to its authenticity. And he and I—yesterday—showed it to the circuit judge."

"It's important, is it? Take it from him, Kyle. Fetch it to me." The ramrod started forward, and the wagon driver jumped down, to hand the rancher the envelope himself.

By now Slocum, wanting to get closer, was edging through the tightly bunched punchers. He squeezed by Harve, Budge, and Juan, but when he tried to move past Wasatch, the old-timer tugged his sleeve and hissed. "Slocum! Y'see Joel Macy standing yonder? Just come outside?"

"I see him joining the crowd."

"He hates your guts, Slocum. Best not turn your back on that 'un."

The bank cashier seemed all ears to the confrontation. And when rancher Cecil unfolded the official-looking foolscap and scanned it, Macy's eyes fixed on his face. The change that came over St. James was striking: His jaw dropped, and his fine-boned but dissipated features blanched. The aristocrat almost staggered. "You claim this is authentic, Parson?" The voice veered high, nearly broke.

"Look at the signature," directed Phineas Garroway. "As I said, it's been verified by Judge Nahum Jones."

St. James slapped the paper. "But this—this *claims* to be Fiona's will—"

Garroway's features carried a sanctimonious smirk. "I advise you to accept the facts, Mr. St. James. To disbelieve availeth you naught."

"This says that you—Phineas Garroway—are my wife's heir! Oh, not her *sole* heir—oh, no! You share the windfall with your flock. Your so-called congregation!" St. James waved the sheet. "How did you say you came by this?"

St. James started for the wagon, but before he'd gone a step, the driver snatched back the document. Kyle Reeve moved to head him off, but now a number of flock members—disciples?—had jumped from their rigs. Although they didn't look menacing, exactly, as they advanced, Slocum had to admit they looked determined—damned determined.

"That document is fake," Cecil St. James roared. "Bloody rot! Look at the date—'twas written just a month ago!"

"Boss—" Kyle Reeve began.

"Out of my way! I'll trounce that goddamned Bible thumper!"

Now two more men were at Cecil St. James's side: Joel Macy and Slocum. Macy was infuriated, Slocum deadly calm. "St. James," he said, "I don't guess you'll stomp anybody in the next minute or two. Look."

Most of the adult males in the wheeled rigs had alighted and moved to station themselves around the wagon on which their leader stood. Most were stolid, strong men of the soil, a few armed with scythes, shovels, or other tools, others displaying pistols or rifles. But more disturbing were a number of more sinister, harder-faced types. These horsemen had just ridden from the rear and were now dismounting. All wore holsters in which well-cared-for six-guns rode, and a few also held wicked-looking shotguns—hammers back.

Joel, talking past St. James, said, "Slocum! We've got to get that will, light a sulfur match, burn it!"

"Whoa, Macy! Think. What claim to the Diamond 7 would that move give *you*?"

The man's swollen, lopsided face contorted. "Hell, there's got to be another will. Maybe an older one! I don't aim to give up my chance for riches!"

Now St. James looked at the husband of his dead wife's cousin, fists clenching and unclenching. "You're a bloody sod, Macy—don't you know it? As if I don't have troubles enough now—"

"What you want us to do, Boss?" one of the ranch hands called. "Unlimber our shootin' irons? Hell, them jaspers be no more'n sodbusters—"

"Sodbusters with scythes and Greeners charged with buck! And they outnumber us two to one!"

"Abner's right," a different cowboy grunted. "Best button your lip, Doyle Bean. I, for one, don't want my ass shot off!"

Slocum wasn't surprised to see St. James's men show yellow streaks. Oh, sure, they'd gotten after *him* like grizzly-mean badasses, but they were basically just punchers. When it came down to it, there was quite a difference between facing a footsore loner and a mob of armed-to-the-teeth land grabbers.

And now the weathervane had swung an about-face. There was small doubt who held the high cards this deal.

Phineas Garroway's eyes glowed with zeal, and his body seemed to expand inside the suit. "Yesterday word got around of Sister Fiona's demise. It seems Mr. Macy informed the sheriff, and the news quickly spread through town. As soon as *I* heard, I dug out this envelope entrusted to me. Imagine my surprise at what it contained! 'Praise be,' I cried, then summoned the flock—"

"That damned gathering we saw at the church," growled Macy.

"—which, convening at a meeting, reached a decision. A decision of what to do with Sister Fiona's bequest. Why, it's proof positive of Providence's bounty to believers."

"And what decision's that?" called Slocum.

"Mr. Slocum, isn't it? Because you befriended Sister at the last, I don't mind answering. The decision reached by the church members is this: That the best thing is to divide the property. First and foremost, this ranch. And do it now, immediately! The people are convinced—and I agree— such is the Lord's blessing—"

"No!"

Heads swiveled. The shouter was Joel Macy.

He rushed on: "I'm onto your shenanigans, Garroway! So you're here to take possession? Divvy up the land? You won't get away with it!" The stringy man lunged through the cordon, then tried to scale the wagon and get at Garroway. Joel's face was an apoplectic purple, his hands desperate, scrabbling claws.

Good thing I took his guns away, Slocum thought. He's been drinking and is a danger to himself.

But there were other dangers to Macy, too. Garroway shouted: "Tom! To my side, son! Your father's threatened!"

A burly young man in worn-but-clean work clothes stepped up and got behind Macy, tiny piggish eyes squinting. Aged about twenty, brutality his long suit, he reversed a

Greener smoothbore, and slammed the butt down to Macy's head. The cashier's hands sprang from the wheel rim; his feet slid from the hub.

He crashed to the earth, where he lay facedown, a trickle of blood staining his dented derby.

"No call for that," Slocum barked, bulling forward.

He was stopped in his tracks, covered by two hardcase bodyguards. Each was armed with a ten-gauge double-barrel: ugly, mean-eyed Tom and an equally young side-kick.

The latter was jug-eared and eyebrowless, his shoulder-length hair the color of greasy tow.

"Take one more step, Slocum, and be blown to Kingdom Come!"

And the one who'd shouted claimed to know all about Kingdom Come.

He was the pious Reverend Phineas Garroway. . . .

16

Slocum's eyes shifted from the gun wielders to the man on the ground alongside Garroway's wagon. Then they lifted from Joel Macy, lying there senseless, to meet those of the hard-faced, bearded reverend.

"Parson, you always play so rough?"

The preacher shrugged. "Perhaps not, but what's done is done. My son Tom is protective of me—a divinely bestowed trait, I'm sure. And Elihu—the light-haired one?—I find him, too, a most devoted follower. Now, Mr. Slocum and Mr. St. James—if you'll step out of the way, these people mean to claim their land."

"And if we don't?" Slocum demanded. "Those disciples of yours, they'll let daylight through us?"

Garroway a man of God? Slocum thought. Hell, he's got more violence in him than most Apaches.

"Let daylight through you?" he said and laughed, affably. "Not necessarily. Not necessarily, at all. Now that you've calmed down, Tom and Elihu will stop pointing their shotguns." To them he directed: "Do it, son. Do it, Elihu. These poor sinners, I believe, now know how their bread's buttered."

As the gun wielders lowered their double-barrels, Reverend Garroway raised his voice: "Hear this, all you Diamond 7 men! I pray that the Good Shepherd sends down a blessing, that we are enabled to pursue the Lord's will . . ."

As the preacher's words rolled from his tongue, St. James hissed into Slocum's ear: "The man's a fanatic—and a killer. And I don't like the look of those followers of his, not even the women."

Slocum did look—again. Indeed the disciples, both male and female, looked stolid and iron-willed. Likely they'd seize this opportunity much as Macy had tried to—as their one chance to raise their humble lot in life.

Maybe some believed strongly in the righteousness of their "prophet."

Slocum took hold of the unconscious Macy, pulled one limp arm over his shoulder, and lifted the man. Answering St. James, he said, "They're a mean-looking outfit, sure. But do you aim to cave in to that black-beard bastard?"

The Englishman's confidence seemed to be scraping the barrel bottom—and slipping lower. "I'm a blue-blooded gentleman-type, Slocum, not a tin hero. And the men I have to back me are no prizes—those who haven't yet slunk off."

Slocum saw Reeve, Harve, Budge, Abner, and Doyle—and that was all. The others *had* all traipsed off, leaving this sorry lot, most of their feistiness converted to hot air. They stood woodenly rooted, witnesses to a game they had no stakes in. Slocum sensed what was on their minds: the skin-saving advantages of lighting a shuck.

St. James went on: "Bugger me for a coward, but I don't want a massacre. Not at risk to my own skin, or with the deaths of other people on my conscience. The signature on that will—I admit it now—looks damnably like Fiona's. What I said before was bleeding tommyrot. The woman *had* been going into town a lot, of late. And at home? Spending the time spouting Garroway-religion-this, Garroway-religion-that, till a man's half-loony."

The Englishman summed up bitterly. "How deucedly like Fiona—to choose this means of getting even."

Then the Britisher raised his voice: "Garroway! Tell your blighters not to shoot. We're backing off, *Reverend.*"

Above Garroway's facial bush gleamed rows of white teeth. The preacher was smiling. "Ah, wisdom. So gratifying to see. Mr. St. James? Mr. Slocum? I shall ask my disciples to remember you at evening devotions."

"Yeah, sure." Slocum, encumbered by Macy, started to back in the direction of the mansion. Cecil walked at his side, as did his foreman, Reeve.

"Oh, one other thing," boomed Garroway. Slocum halted and looked around, to see the preacher, his son, and the others, looking poised to move. "These good people will be fanning out, picking and taking possession of their farm plots. By evening most of the ranch will be staked and claimed. But we're not an overly demanding group, Mr. St. James: Tonight your men may still sleep in their bunkhouse, and tomorrow leave in the morning. And you, Mr. St. James? And the Macys? You'll be given all day tomorrow to vacate. After that, I'll be taking over the main house."

"What about Slocum?" St. James asked.

"Ah, Mr. Slocum, who has no real connection to the Diamond 7. A wayfarer, an Ishmael, who drifts from place to place. So let him drift on off this property—by tonight."

Before mounting the veranda steps, Slocum said to Cecil, "Don't make a fuss on my account. Not if you won't play rough on your own account. You want to cut and run, your tail between your legs? Hell, do it. That'll save your ass, the asses of your hired folks. I aimed all along to ride out anyhow."

"Boss," Kyle Reeve put in. "About the pay owed the boys up through today . . ."

Slocum left St. James and Reeve standing on the steps, discussing chickenshit things as if they mattered. The big man shouldered on inside. Macy, whom he carried, started to groan and come to.

Nadine was in the room. "My God," she cried, hurrying over. "I was watching at the window, heard some things, but missed a lot. What was said out there, John? I mean, besides that nasty preacher's threats? *Has* Garroway found a will of Fiona's, naming him?"

"Oh, he's claiming more heirs than just himself, Nadine. Holding darned good cards, too, are his congregation. Now, watch out, I'm setting your husband down. That couch looks a good place to stretch Joel out."

She grabbed a needlepoint cushion and put it where Joel's head would rest. The woman's face was pinched, but not—Slocum found out—due to her husband. "The preacher's flock in on Fiona's bequests? An outrage! I would've gone out there, only Joel had forbidden me! And when I saw him knocked down, I guess I got scared—"

Slocum's hand stretched to steady the woman. "Take it easy, gal. St. James doesn't see fit to stand up to the pious bastard—pardon my French. Seems the handwriting on his will matches your cousin's. And a judge, it's claimed, has verified as much."

"Judge Jones in town? That doesn't sound good. The man's more a toady than a man of law—he may have been paid off." Now glancing at her husband: "Gracious, what a goose egg! I've got to help Joel come around. Once he's thinking straight, he'll have ideas on Garroway. Yolanda! The smelling salts?"

The housekeeper, who'd ghosted in, now hastened to the kitchen. Nadine knelt by the couch, chafing her husband's wrists. Yolanda returned with a small pewter vial, undid the stopper, and held it under Joel's bruised nose. The man coughed and blinked.

"I left my rifle upstairs," Slocum muttered. "Never should have. Now I've got to traipse on back there—"

"John! Wait!"

Slocum turned and was treated to a look at Nadine's strained face. Christ! he thought. She sounds like a schoolmarm with the pip. But the color in her cheeks does improve her looks more than a little . . . Then, aloud: "Yes'm?"

"About Fiona's estate? "I'm her only blood kin—"

He doggedly shook his head, then crossed to her and put a big hand on each of her square, thin shoulders. He was aware of her body, which he'd never denied was more than a little well formed. "Nadine," he cautioned, "don't lose your head. Use it. Think. You've spent *how* long searching this house? A whole day, almost? Peeping in every nook and cranny, under beds and in hatboxes? Tearing up carpets? And not only in Fiona's quarters, but going cellar to attic with the help of Lupe?"

"I admit it," she said. "I even went through the papers in Cecil's desk. When he'd left for a while to sit in the privy."

"And you found no will, nothing that showed you were entitled to anything?"

"Well-l-l . . . No."

"Like I figured, not a scrap. So face facts, Nadine. Fiona had the right to change her mind, and that's what she must have done. Decided at some point to leave her property to somebody else, not you. Nadine, without a nailed-down, certified last will and testament, you'd not have gotten the ranch, not even squashed Cecil's claim. So if the place goes to a bunch of religious nuts, so what? What have you lost?"

The woman, sad-faced, shook her head from side to side. Today she'd not done her hair up tightly at her nape. The less severe style was lots more becoming. In fact, now—in her vulnerable state—she didn't look half-bad . . .

Hold on, Slocum, he thought. She's married, and her husband is in the house. The house? Hell, he's in this very same room!

He smiled at her, and started for the staircase.

"John, you say you're going up?"

"I did, and I am. To collect my possibles, since I'm moving out."

"I'll come along with you. Lupe was looking for me. I need to ask her . . . some things."

They parted at the head of the stairs. In the room where he'd spent time enjoying Lupe, Slocum set about gathering up his gear. He didn't like Phineas Garroway, or his son Tom, or their gang of holy rollers—and wouldn't have even if they'd come peaceable, left their guns setting at home against the next prairie chicken hunt. Plainly, the folks didn't act too nice under any circumstances. There had been a time when Slocum would have gone on prod, but this whole St. James affair had become a fiasco.

No more, and no less.

Cecil St. James was determined to back down, gutless and outflanked by a loudmouthed, pushy preacher.

Of course, it appeared the preacher had actually inherited the ranch.

Hard to believe, but Slocum had given in to a heap of heavy evidence.

In a case like this, not even Slocum's own code justified hanging around, defending his personal, maybe cockeyed, brand of honor . . .

17

Slocum sat for more than a few minutes on the soft bed in the ranch-house guest room, dwelling half the time on Socorro, Billy Linn, and horse-raising, the other half on Lupe—partaker with him, on this very spot, of an entire night of whoop-and-holler, hell-for-leather sex play. Lupe's screwing had been the best he'd had in months—with the possible exception of that done with willing, sweet-tailed Dottie Weston.

Ah, the Ophir saloon and fancy house. . . .

Ah, Dottie's quaking rope bed, with its occupant, the rollicking, man's meat–devouring saloon gal. . . .

Finally Slocum told himself: All that's in yesterday, fella. Time to get a move on, drift south. Grab yourself a last sip of Cecil St. James's whiskey, and then ride out. You're coming out ahead, even counting Blue Flame as an even swap—which, of course, he's way more than. Plus that cash money paid you by the Macy couple. I wonder—do they figure they might've gotten their greenbacks' worth?

With his Winchester slung under his arm, Slocum went on back downstairs. He saw neither Lupe, Nadine, nor Yolanda Ramirez, which didn't bother him; in fact, it was no small relief. Thinking of Yolanda reminded him of all the questions he'd posed, and heard no answers for. Perhaps he would never hear those answers.

For example, was the housekeeper's husband, Manuel,

killed on purpose? In cold blood?

If so, by whom?

Yolanda herself? Or Kyle Reeve, possibly jealous of Manuel's status as Fiona's lover?

Or Cecil St. James, Fiona's husband—but also at the time the frequent bedmate of the sultry, big-breasted housekeeper?

Of course, still another possibility existed. Might not St. James and Reeve have been in cahoots, teamed-up on the slaying?

Yet, if the owner and his foreman had been rivals for Fiona at one time, how come Reeve had elected to stay on at the Diamond 7—or been permitted to?

Because St. James wasn't able to oust him?

Was blackmail involved? If so, who was blackmailing whom?

Slocum tossed his Winchester on the vacant couch, which Joel Macy no longer occupied. God only knew where the cashier had taken himself off to. The big man crossed to the sideboard. He felt entitled—perfectly so—to one last drink before he rode out.

Then Cecil walked in, a slurred curse rolling from his twisted lips. "Bloody sod! The last of my Napoleon brandy gone—the best of all m'boozes. I polished off one bottle m'self, Slocum, but there was another—and now it's vanished."

"Joel?"

St. James managed to stagger over to the mantel and prop up his sagging, drunken frame. "Who else but Macy could've t-took it, Slocum, old man? Ra-*ther*! B-bloo-oody, damned s-sod."

It figured that St. James would get drunk, developments being what they were. His easy life—the thing he cherished most—was coming to an end. Why, he might actually have to go out and find himself an honest job.

Slocum stepped to the sideboard, selected a decanter

of aged-in-the-wood sour-mash bourbon, and took a long pull directly from the bottle. The alcohol burned all the way down and lay in a warm pool in the depths of his appreciative stomach.

Good stuff.

He reckoned it would do him for a while.

But he was not permitted to relax for long: Through the open window, he heard the clatter of hooves and a buggy's clickety-clacking rattle. Joel Macy's fly rolled past just outside, the team moving in a trot, the cashier alone on the seat, swaying as if drunk—which he most likely was.

Chipmunk-cheeked Tom, the preacher's son, and albino-like, unsmiling Elihu—the guards on duty—let the bank man pass. Once beyond the ranch gate, Joel took the turn in the road leading toward Antelope Creek.

"He's gone," Slocum said.

"The bounder! He went off forgetting his wife, leaving her here."

"True. Nadine must be around someplace."

"Bloody h-hell!" St. James grabbed the bottle that Slocum had set down, put it to his lips, and gulped—and gulped.

The Brit's Adam's apple bobbed like a fisherman's cork. Then he joined Slocum at the window, and together the oddly matched pair watched the activity out there.

Things were moving rapidly, free of the usual workmen's din of shouts and curses.

Garroway's true believers were going about quietly and industriously staking their claims. Aside from an eerie lack of noise, the Diamond 7 had taken on the aspect of a bustling gold-strike gulch. The disciples were like prospectors in search of the mother lode—a little crazy, a little overeager, and showing it.

From the mansion to the encircling high ground—and Slocum supposed, beyond—men were sighting, marking distances, heaving boulder boundary markers, driving stakes. Some women, muscles straining and sunbonnets wagging, were engaged in rolling wagons into place, just so. Others, together with children, toiled at pitching tents, kindling camp fires, tending livestock, and a hundred other campers' tasks.

The favored farm sites had access to the stream, and Slocum saw some arguments under way, complete with shouts and arm waving. In the distance one man knocked another down, attracting the attention of the gorilla-armed peacekeeper, Elihu.

The albino ran over, snarled a few words, and the dispute subsided.

None of which was lost to St. James, even intoxicated as he was. "Look at those bounders, S-Slocum. In a few months they'll have this whole range plowed and planted with crops. Partitioned with fences, I have no doubt. The land will be ruined, no longer fit, even to run cattle. Not enough rain in this country for agriculture. The winds'll play hell with the topsoil."

"No doubt of it, St. James. Why not change your mind, hold onto the ranch till the matter of the will can be taken to court? Then hire lawyers for your fighting?"

"Haven't you noticed, Slocum? I'm a coward and a worthless bugger, unable to stand up to Garroway now, today? To hell with this ranch! And to hell with that woman!" The Englishman reeled back, lifted the decanter, and hurled it at the painting of Fiona. The picture was dashed to the floor, liquor splashing across bright pigments, dissolving some, changing others. The reds ran as if transformed to blood.

And over the ripped canvas and split gilt frame, St. James—the damned fool—stood in his silk shirt, his shoulders heaving.

Sobbing the sobs of the mentally-racked intoxicated.

"I reckon you *are* better off away from here," said Slocum. "Too many reminders, St. James. Too much guilt to deal with."

"I-I didn't kill Fiona."

"I know that. You were screwing Yolanda at the time of the ambush. Spent all midday that day with the Mexican woman. Lupe told me."

"Nor did I *have* my wife killed."

"St. James, I believe you."

"Then who—?"

Slocum shrugged. "I hate to say it, but it hardly matters. The damage is done. In a few days Garroway will move into the mansion, start living like a sultan, sell off the Diamond 7 cattle he doesn't choose to keep. Next year when the crops come in—such as they might—he'll find a way to enforce kickbacks from each and every flock member. If he's a man of God, I'm Sitting Bull's grandnephew! I glimpsed greed in that jasper's eyes, St. James—something I know when I see it."

"I should've seen all the blather coming, hey, old chap? All Fiona's talking fondly of Garroway of late."

Christ, thought Slocum. Tears were actually poised at the Brit's eye corners.

Slocum assayed Cecil's condition and decided to run a classic poker bluff. "Oh, by the way, St. James—a minute ago I brought up guilt, and noticed you didn't balk at the word. *Were* you in on Ramirez's death together, you and Reeve? I know Manuel was a human stud, servicing Fiona and Yolanda, both. And with *Kyle* fancying your wife, and *you* fancying Manuel's wife—"

St. James stared with bleak eyes. In their depths, since Slocum's words, there showed more than a trace of soberness, after all. "I'll tell you, Slocum, but this mustn't go any farther. If you blab what I say, I'll swear you're lying through your teeth. But, yes, Kyle and I did get together, do in the sodding wretch. I planned it; my less-cowardly accomplice did the actual manhandling. After Reeve clubbed Manuel, together we threw him in the wild stallion's stall." St. James waved his hand dismissively. "Oh, not Blue Flame, a different horse. But with regard to Kyle's staying here, he was a decently qualified foreman, and he and I were never jealous of each other. Anyhow, Fiona never welcomed Reeve back to her bed. Some rot about her love for her vaquero living in her memory."

"St. James, you're a helluva storyteller," Slocum breathed.

"And such raconteurship—believe me, Slocum—makes for a dry throat." The Englishman stalked to the liquor array and made his selection potent Taos Lightning. This, too, he drank straight from the bottle.

Slocum passed through the hall toward the kitchen, and glimpsed a flash of color. The same red as Yolanda's dress. The housekeeper had been listening, then. But so what? She had to have known before now that her husband had been murdered.

On the kitchen table Slocum found a sizeable chunk of ham and three fresh biscuits. These he took charge of, wrapping the food in a large napkin and carrying it in the hand not burdened with a rifle.

Hell, it's late in the day for starting out, he thought, and I doubt Fiona would've sent a man away on an empty stomach. A too-well-brought-up and too polite lady is how I sized her up in the short time I knew her.

Exiting by the back way, the big man did not see Lupe. So there were no farewells to be said. Just as well. He strode to the corral and threw his saddle on Blue Flame, cinched up tight, booted his Winchester, and stuffed the grub into a saddlebag.

Then he swung aboard. He trotted the animal around behind the barn, then up the hillside behind the buildings cluster. No sodbusters, as it happened, had yet chosen to park themselves there.

He was bound for Socorro at last, but he had one more stop to make.

One that shouldn't take him long.

A minute or two, at most. . . .

18

Reining in the gray under canopying oaks and elders, Slocum dismounted at the place described to him by Wasatch, then moved ahead on foot around the caboose-size boulder, to the edge of the ranch burial ground. As he'd expected, the site contained old graves—maybe as many as seven or eight, although just two had markers. The older of these was of stone, tilted at a sharp angle, discolored and covered with a layer of greenish-brown lichen.

The newer marker was the board that old Wasatch had been carving earlier that day. He had obviously completed the work, chiseling Fiona's name and dates, then hobbled out here and set up the remembrance. There it stood now— at one end of a recently turned rectangle of red earth.

There was no way to guess which of the older graves was that of Manuel Ramirez—even if Slocum wanted to.

As Wasatch had mentioned, the ranch hands who'd laid Fiona to rest had erected a fence around the forlorn mound of clods.

But another person had beaten Slocum to the site, and the presence drew him up with a start. A woman in a dark dress stood beside Fiona's last resting place, hands clasped and head bowed reverently. Slocum recognized the dress, recognized the narrow, high, square shoulders, the color of the soft brown hair coiled into a bun in back, even though the owner faced the other way.

Not hearing his approach, however, Nadine Macy didn't turn. Slocum, permitting her moment of quiet at the grave of her dead cousin, quietly drew a cigar—one of his own, this time. Lighting up, he drew in the smoke he enjoyed, then exhaled the first lungful in a bluish, hazy rush.

Then Slocum softly cleared his throat, causing Nadine to whirl and look at him.

Her appearance was bad—surprisingly so—and Slocum showed his anger, lean jaw clenched and working. One of Nadine's eyes was nearly closed by purple swelling, and besides the black eye, a trickle of blood had dried and crusted at the corner of her split lip. Somebody had used his fists on the woman, and although Slocum had seen females who'd suffered worse, now he felt bile surge in his gullet.

"What happened?" he blurted, dropping the smoke, toeing out the coal. He guessed her answer before she gave it. "Joel did this to you?"

A nod. "Yes. Joel."

"He pounded on you, then drove off, left you abandoned out here on the Diamond 7?"

She wiped her better eye, although no tear had shown itself. "He was crazy-mad, John, when he regained consciousness. You know, after being knocked out by Garroway's henchman. Yolanda and I couldn't control him. He found Cecil's brandy bottle. A few long drinks, then he ordered me to go outside with him. Out back of the house, out of sight . . . well, you can see—"

Slocum inspected the swollen areas and the cuts, tilting her head from side to side. His diagnosis: painful, but not serious. Nadine would heal, and heal quickly. But she was one spooked filly, and was going to require some gentling down. "Yeah, I see what your husband's fists can do. You'll live—but maybe not as his wife any longer? Haven't you had enough of that son of a bitch?"

She tugged from him and sat on a weathered pine stump, hugging herself. "Joel is definitely *not* a good man—he has his weaknesses. One of those is ambition, aggravated because he's never made a success of himself. He hates his job, that of glorified clerk. When this inheritance thing came up, he jumped at it—like me. Of course, it was wrong to count chickens before they hatched, and it led to grief— my grief. When things fell through, Joel simply took out his frustration on me."

"You had reason to suspect you might not be an heir?"

"Yes." A pause. Then: "May I confide in you, John Slocum? Unburden myself?"

"Why not? I've likely guessed part of it already."

When she started talking, she droned on softly, as if she were controlling herself, keeping deep emotion at bay. Slocum listened, sensing how much she was in need of a listener. "John, that deep, dark secret hinted at by Cecil in the parlor? It's not much of a secret, though I confess, it's dark enough, and I'm ashamed now. The worst of it happened years and years ago. When I was growing up, I lived in Waltham, Massachusetts—the same little city as Fiona's family: her, her parents, and her brother. Fiona's people were rich—her daddy owned factories for the manufacture of cloth. As for me, I felt like a poor relation, which I was."

She coughed into her hand, then went on more slowly. "I hate to say it, John, but when I got old enough to attract men, I became rather wild. I rouged my cheeks and dressed immodestly—not as lately, in plain styles. I flirted with old society gents and young ones: It sort of gave me power, you see—made me feel not poor. And yes, I went to bed with different fellows back in those days— more than a few."

Nadine didn't raise her eyes, but she went on. "Well, that's the basis of my notorious reputation. Word about me got around, even followed me when I tried to leave it behind, came out west. Cecil found out. But the worst part Cecil never learned. Nor did Fiona know—at least for quite a while. When I moved to Antelope Creek and married Joel, she befriended me. But then, two months or so ago—it seems—she received a letter—"

Nadine Macy fixed Slocum with a stricken look. "Oh, John, I just found out today! The letter turned up when I was searching Fiona's bureau, looking for a will."

Slocum spoke carefully. "I take it this letter is the reason she changed her will? Decided to leave her property to the Garroway crowd?"

"Yes. It was a deathbed letter from a spiteful person we'd known back in Waltham. It told Fiona that I was responsible for her brother's suicide. And years ago, after Fiona had come out here, but while her father was still alive, Douglas, her brother, *had* chosen to end his life. Hanged himself with a drapery pull in the old family manse. Well, it's true that I'd seduced him—he was handsome, dashing—and could he ever dance the schottische! But I couldn't stick with one fellow, not the way I was then. So, like a butterfly, I flitted on to my next conquest. I never expected the results to be so . . . so tragic!"

"You don't need to tell me more, Nadine. But this explains a lot. For example, why you came here this afternoon to say good-bye to Fiona."

"John, since Garroway's inheriting came to light, I've realized a thing or two. Mainly, how natural it was that Fiona fell under his spell. He has the good looks, the smooth manners, when he feels like showing them. Plus the magnetism, that voice that can send shivers up women's spines—"

A twig snapped in the woods off to the right. Slocum turned that way, his hand clutching the butt of his Colt.

But he didn't draw the gun when he heard the rich, deep voice boom out: "Ah, Mr. Slocum. And is that Mrs. Macy with you? It is, if I'm not mistaken."

Slocum relaxed as Phineas Garroway stepped from behind a noble cedar. The two men keeping him company—Tom

and Elihu—seemed on their good behavior now. No shotguns were in evidence, and their six-guns were holstered,
their hands swinging easily at their sides.

Nadine got to her feet, but Slocum did the talking. "Just
stopped up here, Garroway, on our way to clearing off your
spread."

"A nice gesture, to be sure, paying last respects. However, as far as today is concerned . . ." The preacher's eyes
rose to the sky in the west, where the colors were already
bleeding into the hues of sunset: clouds turned orange,
streaked with blood-red. The low, pumpkin-colored sun
cast long shadows of people, trees, the old and the new
grave markers.

As the preacher stroked his beard and talked, Tom and
Elihu, apparently curious, moved to the new grave-marker.
Tom strolled to the fence, beyond which several inches
of turned earth extended, not careful where he put his
feet. "Well, Garroway," Slocum addressed the preacher,
"I reckon it *is* time we ought to get moseying."

Slocum glanced down. He saw the footprints pressed by
Tom in loose grave clods.

The heelprints didn't match.

Now, just what might that mean?

Slocum looked more closely at the young man's boots.
Tom's right bootheel gleamed with fresh polish—in fact,
on careful inspection, it was clear that the heel had recently
been replaced by a cobbler!

Which suggested that the original heel might have been
shot off, perhaps as the owner was fleeing from the scene
of a murder. . . .

Damn, thought Slocum. The jasper's body build looks
familiar, too, the more I eyeball him.

"Yes, Mr. Slocum, you *had* best be on your way. The
sentries I'm posting will soon secure the premises—"

"Maybe before we leave, Garroway, you'd be willing to
answer a question?" Had the preacher's face darkened, or

was it just the changing light? "On the other hand, maybe now isn't such a good time, after all."

Slocum took Nadine's shoulder and urged her down the path toward where—out of sight from this spot—he'd left Blue Flame tied.

Slocum felt it less than safe to turn his back. Garroway had noticed him studying the footprints. And if the preacher wanted to hold onto the ranch, could he afford to let a man suspicious of him just walk away?

A character like Slocum?

Of one thing Slocum was more than sure: Tom definitely wasn't the type to act on his own. If it had been he who'd shot down Fiona, he'd been following orders. Now, in front of Slocum, at the foot of the grave mound of Fiona St. James, the three men likely involved in the woman's killing stood. There was Tom, with twisted, twitching lips. Then Elihu, with the colorless, glassy eyes and pale, stringy hair.

And finally, there was the towering, black-bearded Phineas. The mastermind.

"Come on along, John," Nadine said casually. "Good day, Reverend. Good day, gentleman."

About then, all hell broke loose.

Things started happening more quickly than the eye could follow: Slocum's right hand dipped for his Colt, while at the same time he threw himself into a dive to his left. Nadine he shoved ahead of him, stumbling. With space opened between him and the woman, Slocum spun, crawfished and dropped to a squared-off gunman's stance. His opponents went for their pistols also, and because they stood well apart, things looked bad for Slocum.

Still, the cards had been dealt, and the hand had to be played out, not merely pondered on. . . .

The race to get guns drawn was close—perilously so.

Slocum's thumb jerked back the hammer of the Colt, and his index finger started to stroke the trigger—even before his three remaining fingers completely freed the gun from the holster. Forearm and revolver coming level, his cool aim was from the hip. All this was the result of years of practice, by a man peculiarly gifted in the six-gun art. Elihu's revolver was up and already cocked as Slocum dropped the hammer.

Slocum's shot was hasty, by necessity. The report of the .44–40 sang, and smoke mushroomed from the barrel.

Nadine Macy squawked and dove for cover.

Elihu took the bullet in his abdomen, several inches to the right of center, and was slapped violently backward. Meanwhile Tom's and the parson's shots hummed harmlessly past Slocum. Elihu reeled into the fence, knocking it down, his pistol dropping from his fingers.

And then he flopped across the grave, to lie hugging his wound and kicking.

As Slocum recocked with lightning speed, the senior Garroway flourished his Harrington & Richardson sawhandle pistol—and crabbed to his left. "Get him, Tom! Get him!" The small .32-caliber went off with a dull *pop*. Another miss. Slocum's second shot blew the hat from the head of the quick-moving preacher.

Tom, shooting at Slocum, also missed—and on his third try, his six-gun jammed. He flung the weapon at Slocum, irreligiously cursing. The parson, also forgetting himself, yelled: "He's killed Elihu, Tom! Damn it, let's save our own hides while we can!"

So saying, he ran into the trees, Tom at his heels, legs pumping like steam pistons.

The graveyard was again quiet.

Nadine sat on the ground, dazed, as Slocum ran up. "Woman, you hurt?"

"I-I seem to be. My leg." She hiked up her skirt to her knee, permitting Slocum to see the damage, which looked more painful than serious. Her left shin showed broken skin and oozing blood, and a bit of swelling was setting in.

"Looks like a ricochet split a rock, and a chunk flew, barked that ankle. Can you walk?"

"I can try."

He grabbed her arm and tugged her up. "We've got to clear out. Tom is Fiona's killer—*I* know it, and he and his pappy know that I know it. And when they come back, it'll be with a gang of those sentries Parson Garroway mentioned—"

"Slocum! Over here, S-Slocum!" The call, accompanied by a peculiar, whining series of doglike coughs, came from Elihu. Elihu had hiked himself into an awkward, half-sitting position, propped against the slab of carved wood that marked Fiona's grave. Slocum strode over to the man, noting the pool of blood he sat in. His breathing was labored, his face the color of rancid suet.

He appealed: "Can't you get help for me? I'm beggin' y'all. A doc?"

Slocum shook his head, at the same time punching fresh loads into his six-gun. If the albino had looked ugly of face and form before, he now looked ghastly. "No dice, Elihu. A doc couldn't save you, even if there was one close enough to get here in time. You're gut-shot. Aren't you feeling cold about now, but with a great old fire roaring deep in your belly? And pain? Big, big pain?"

A nod. A groan.

Nadine had hobbled up beside Slocum, her hurt foot held clear of the ground as she leaned against him. He put a calming hand on the arm of the woman. "You haven't got long," he told the wounded man. "Want to tell us about who killed the St. James woman?"

With much effort and wincing, Elihu blurted it out. "It was the fake preacher's plan—him who I came to know years back, when I was a kid and a snot-nose. Hell, Garroway ran a medicine show outa a circus wagon, peddled snake oil town-to-town, all over Kansas. Then he come to Antelope Creek, preached them fire-and-brimstone sermons, and found the suckers lovin' it. Especially them as ever worked on farms. Garroway had a notion, too, to snag him a rich female—and by God, he done it."

The man was gasping and panting as he talked, becoming weaker by the minute as his life drained away. His face grimaced with successive waves of pain, but he went on in a low, feeble voice. "Garroway started screwin' with Miz St. James, claimed he'd get hitched with her, weren't she married already. But she allus put off decidin'. Then, two months back she changed her will, made the preacher heir—or so she claimed. 'That tears it,' says Garroway! All this stuff, Slocum, the preacher told his son, Tom. And Tom—on account of me 'n' him's friends—let on t'me the whole sorry yarn."

Nadine tried to sum it up: "So, Tom, on his father's orders, ambushed Fiona from Breadloaf Bluff? In order that Garroway'd get the inheritance? But as it turned out, she'd allotted shares to the congregation—didn't that rile him?"

"Oh, h-he c-carried on some, but . . ." Weak and reedy, the words trailed off.

Slocum gently turned Nadine away. Elihu's stomach was apparently pumping blood—mouthfuls of it were brimming over and down the man's chin, staining the lower part of his face red, sickening to behold. From deep in the towhead's chest, gasping death rattles began to issue. All at once his chin dropped to his chest and his mouth went slack and gaping. Frosted, empty eyes showed between his half-closed lids.

"He's dead, Nadine," Slocum said. "Let's stir our stumps. We'll have to ride double aboard Blue Flame, avoid the risky ranch yard, get away over the back ridge."

"My ankle, John. It hurts and feels weak."

Unceremoniously he picked her up, half-running up the path.

Now that they knew of the preacher and his son's guilt, there was no time to waste. Slocum had let the shoot-out die down, choosing not to risk the life of the unarmed woman.

But that didn't mean Slocum would let the Garroways' crimes drop—not by a long shot. But he'd do his getting even at a time of his own choosing.

With—unless he missed his guess—his Colt and Winchester blazing.

19

"Here's a likely looking spot to hole up. What do you think of it?" Slocum reined in the hard-loping gray stud at the clearing's edge, half-turning in the saddle to glance back at Nadine.

The woman perched behind the cantle, skirts tucked between her tender skin and horsehide, peered around Slocum. What she saw was a small, foliage-screened clearing. She and Slocum had ridden over the high ground to the west of Diamond 7 headquarters, where the terrain was the roughest for miles—as her sore rump could testify. Nadine was sweaty and dusty, her bun of hair in back listing far to starboard. Other brown tresses spilled down the dress front, thrust out by her full breasts.

"You're right about one thing, John: We should stop here. I'm exhausted, hungry, and my ankle keeps twingeing. I can't go any farther right now."

"I'm liking that notch over there for spreading out bedrolls," Slocum announced. "A cold camp and a dry one— no fire or flowing water. It's the safest way to go, Nadine. Savvy?"

"But we've got a canteen, haven't we? I mean, we're bound to be thirsty."

"Maybe there'll be a comfortable amount of water. The horse drinks first, though—out of my hat. He's worked pretty hard."

Nadine made a face as he dismounted from in front of her, then helped her down, too. When her left foot hit the ground, the ankle bent and pangs shot up her calf, fully as annoying as back at the ranch graveyard. Slocum could now see swelling above her shoe. Nadine took an experimental step or two—limping—then stood and surveyed the surroundings. The woods were pine mixed with aspen, the tree leaves and needled branches golden in the rays of the dying sun.

The man and woman were bone-weary, an aftermath of the gunplay and the ride, so rest would be welcome. Garroway and his gunmen—the so-called "guards"—shouldn't be able to find them; that was why Slocum had picked this place. It would soon be dark—and no camp fire meant not a trace of smoke that might give away their hideout.

"I'll get unsaddled and picket the horse. And I've got grub, Nadine, pilfered from Yolanda's kitchen."

Nadine said, "Poor Yolanda. Having to put up with stuffy, British Cecil, now that he's going to be without the ranch."

"You reckon she'll stay with the limey? He's a drinker, Nadine, not to mention a loafer and a yellow-belly."

She sighed. "I stuck with Joel, didn't I? At least, while there was still hope."

In the fading light of sunset he studied her features. The facial swelling from her husband's beating had started to go down, and most of the pain she was now feeling, he surmised, was the result of her barked ankle. "But you're over your husband finally, I reckon. After he beat on you the way he did, then drove off in the buggy, leaving you in the lurch."

She gingerly fingered her face. "I allow it—I can't stand to lay eyes on the man. No, John, Joel will never get near me again. Not where I'm going."

"And where'll that be?"

She looked beyond Slocum, to where the evening star

hung in the purple sky. "Oh, far away."

Then her gaze returned to Slocum's. "Oh, all right," she admitted, "I don't know, really, where I'll end up. Can you live with that tonight, John?"

He worked at undoing the horse's cinches, and when they were loose, he proceeded to the latigos. As he slid the saddle from Blue Flame's back, he assured her: "I can live with whatever you say—with food on my stomach. Care to get busy laying out that grub?"

"I'll do it directly, John. Only, I've been up on Blue Flame for quite a while, as you know. I'm needing now to heed a call of nature."

When she said that, it was Slocum's turn to shrug.

First Nadine had torn her lower petticoat into cotton strips, and then Slocum had bandaged her ankle. Leaving her shoe unbuttoned left room. Next, they'd split the ham and biscuits into four sparse portions and wrapped half in oilcloth, ready to serve as tomorrow's breakfast. The rest of the morsels they'd wolfed into their mouths, using their fingers, then washed the food down with swallows of lukewarm canteen water.

Finished, Slocum sat back against a deadfall, grunting his satisfaction. It being too dark by now to try and clean his guns, he rolled a quirly, half by feel, the rest by gosh-and-by-golly.

The sulfur match flared as he lit up, and he was able to see Nadine clearly for a brief half minute. The meal and the sitting in one place for a while had picked her up, but she still could use repose, he reckoned. But when the match burned out, she offered: "I noticed you noticing me, John. I'm afraid I don't look too good—my face, my hair. My portmanteau, it got left back at the mansion. My brush and comb are in it—"

"You look just fine, Nadine. But the important thing now," he insisted, "is to get some shut-eye. Give that hurt ankle of yours a chance to heal as best it can. Tomorrow could be a busy day."

Nadine frowned, her face to Slocum a pale orb in the weak light. "For some reason, that doesn't sound as cheering as it ought. Won't we simply be able to swing past Antelope Creek and tell the sheriff what we've discovered about Fiona's murder? That Garroway was responsible? And after turning the matter over to the law, I'd like to buy a riding horse and start off with you when you head for Socorro. You'll let me keep you company, won't you, John—as far as the railroad line there? Only a big locomotive, for sure, will be able to go far and fast enough to suit this girl. I've a peck of forgetting to do."

His smile was tight. "You say 'simple,' Nadine, but it can't be simple. For a whole nosebag full of reasons. Never mind that that tin star Van Eaton doesn't like me much, and won't care to take our word about the killings. There's more: I've got a code, sort of, although I allow that at times like this it might not sound too sensible. Part of it's about taking money for a failed job—which is why I aim to repay most of the hundred you gave me. You'll need it for train fare, sounds like."

She started to protest, but he went on: "Then there's Garroway. True, no real *close* friends of mine have gotten done in by him—only Fiona, who I scarcely knew. But what I *do* have against the preacher—and his son—is this: They tried to put me six feet under today, in the same graveyard where the shoot-out was played. If I know their kind, they won't rest till they do kill me. And they'll want to shut you up for keeps, too, Nadine. They'll guess that if I figured out from the bootprint that they killed Fiona, I'd share the news with you. And as for taking lives, those two are as cold-blooded as they come."

"I know it," she said. "Fiona trusted Garroway and put him in her will. But when she signed that paper, she signed her death warrant." A sigh, and then: "So, Garroway and company will be coming after us? Likely with those body-guards of his? Lordy, John, we should've kept riding through the night!"

Slocum disagreed. "You couldn't have gone any further, gal. You were so tuckered, you'd have fallen off Blue Flame. And it's never good to ride one's horse till it founders. That big stud, he's been carrying double—a hell of a job. Anyhow, Garroway's boys can't do much tracking on a night with no moon."

"But they *will* be after us tomorrow, come daylight?"

"Bet on it, Nadine. Bet on it."

"You plan an ambush, don't you, rather than a run? That's your style, to stand and fight. I'll tell you something, John: I can handle a gun." He could hear her squirming around, making her outstretched leg more comfortable. "I was thinking a minute ago, how it's too bad, in a way. Too bad not to have people fighting on our side. Like the Mexicans from the ranch—but they cleared out as soon as Cecil threw in the sponge. Or Cecil and Reeve—but those two are cowards, aren't they, John? Men who can't be depended on?"

Slocum finished his smoke, rose, and went to fetch blankets from his saddle roll. "Nadine, we'd best relax during the hours we have left. Get some shut-eye."

"You'll waken early, John?"

"The birds, they're up and singing before sunup every day."

They got the two blankets spread on the ground—yards apart—with Nadine hopping around, sparing her poorly ankle. Finally they both lay down. Slocum tugged off his boots, placed his Colt and gunbelt on a rock beside his head, then pulled half his cover over him.

After a short time, the rustling when the horse moved as he grazed was the only noise that broke the night quiet.

Slocum dozed.

• • •

When he opened his eyes again, King Night still reigned. Slocum's surroundings were washed in inky blackness, dark as an underground mine stope. He became aware of Nadine crouching near his head, her unbound hair loose around her face, that face mere inches from his.

"It's me, John. May I join you?"

Slocum's answer was to shift to the edge of his blanket, making room. Nadine raised the cover and slipped herself under. Except for her ankle bandage, it felt as if she'd removed all her clothes.

He hadn't removed his.

Damn!

As she settled in, she contrived to press her body to his. "I was too jittery to sleep, John, what with the twinges in my poor, hurt leg."

"You don't reckon you and me will be bumping it, making it worse?"

"Anything we might do would only take my mind off it, John. That'd be good."

He sniffed the fragrance of her. "*You're* good."

"You're good, too, John Slocum. You've taught me things today—about what a real man is." Nadine snuggled her body even closer, pillowing breasts, voluptuous hips, and smooth thighs pressing him.

Slocum let his hands have their way, and they started roaming. Nadine was soft all over, and he let his palm slide down her back, enjoying every inch he covered. When he reached her buttocks, he found their yielding amazingly erotic.

By now, predictably, he felt a swelling in his groin. He knew what was coming next, and so did his burgeoning sexual tool.

Nadine Macy sighed, her fingers busy with his buttons. She opened his shirt and peeled it off, and then her hands spidered downward across his bared chest. She climbed onto her hands and knees, whispering, "If I'm on top, it'll bother me less." A giggle. "Of course, I mean my ankle." Her swaying breasts brushed his mat of chest hairs as she leaned above him. Her lips came down on his mouth, her tongue probing until it gained its entrance. Slocum opened his mouth to hers, and her hands fled to his waist, flew to opening his lower garments.

He arched his spine upward as she stripped off his trousers and long flannels.

Seeking his penis, she found it fully hard.

"Lordy, John, you're big!"

His organ throbbed in answer.

"You're going to fill me, John Slocum, like I've never been filled! And, believe me, I'm aching for it." She dragged his rampant manhood to bury it in the silky fur of her lower tummy.

Slocum felt his balls filling up, and he groaned in the night. His hands sought her breasts, and as he fondled them he felt her bullet-shaped nipples harden. Nadine Macy reached around and pressed his head, guiding his mouth from one sweet-tasting, pebbly nipple area to the other. All the while she quivered delightedly, laughing low and continuing to clutch his hard, twitching flagpole.

He reached up to roll her over.

"No," she whispered above him. "Just lie still."

He did as commanded. She lifted a leg and eased it over his thighs, then settled sensuously and maddeningly down on his lower torso. Her hand still gently clasped his cock. Her tongue was alive now, darting with abandon. From his throat to his earlobes, from his right nipple to his left, it fluttered and flicked.

Slocum's desire mounted, and Nadine Macy sensed it.

It was time for *her* to mount *him*.

Slowly, slowly, she lowered her crotch, Slocum feeling first its outer, moist caress, then as she pushed down, her hungry, slick vagina swallowing his shaft.

Nadine's inner heat sent waves of sensation radiating through him.

She moaned gently as she squirmed, contracting around him as he swelled within her. Slocum reached up to grasp her buttocks and drive upward with his reaming cock.

She was leaning forward, motionless, in welcome, and then she began to rock, obviously enjoying herself to the hilt. Slocum met her movements with a sharp upthrust. "Yes," she cried breathlessly. "Yes, John, so long and big around! I love it!"

"You're as hot as they come," he hissed into her ear, because he found her so. The great cushions that were her breasts swayed and slapped his face, and the sensation was maddening. With a strangled wail, Nadine spread her legs to further impale herself, while Slocum increased the urgency of his pumping drives. The tempo of his grinding brought her to frantic writhings of her hips. He sensed her climax approaching.

Slocum didn't slow and he didn't flag, and soon he felt the woman shuddering, bearing down. "More! Oh, more!" she pleaded. The man did her bidding. Now he made vocal sounds of his own—guttural ones—as he drew his penis farther back down and plunged upward again ever faster, ever harder. Delightedly speared as she was, she writhed and pushed . . . and came!

Slocum kept his eyes squeezed shut, leaned back. She was working on him now, grinding, so that he lost all track of time. The point of no return was reached, and there was no more holding back. He'd felt Nadine's frantic spasmings earlier, and now again she was quivering top to toe, tremblingly clawing at his back as if the world were spinning, coming to an end. He understood: She was reaching a second peak of ecstasy. Then he rammed upward with all his energies and allowed himself sweet release, as Nadine's gasps of rapture broke the night quiet.

The woman's head dropped to Slocum's chest; her form

sank and glued itself to his, connected by their fleshy bond. The ecstasy and the frenzy waned, and the pair nestled, their muscles and nerves relaxed.

Fleecy clouds of drowsiness settled around, and when they slumbered, it was soundly and without dreams.

20

"My God, John! Less than an hour from breaking camp this morning and riding out—and here *they* come? And us caught by surprise, so far away from town and safety?"

From where Slocum and Nadine were trotting along on Blue Flame, the distant horsemen seemed to be heading their way, it was true. And coming from the direction of the Diamond 7, which gave a pretty strong clue as to their identity. There looked to be five or six of them, indistinct forms because of distance and a masking cloud of hoof-stirred, drifting dust.

Bearing as the riders were, following the course of a tree-lined stream, they stood to cut off Slocum and Nadine from town—and any chance of the woman riding on alone to bring back reinforcements for the fight that might be in store. Slocum brought the gray to a skittish halt under the brow of the hill to avoid being skylined, even for a moment, against the sweep of brilliant morning blue. "I doubt they've spotted us, Nadine—and I don't aim to let 'em just now." Then he told her, "Hang on. Let's get out of sight behind those trees yonder."

They rode fast along the tree line, the thick buffalo grass muffling Blue Flame's heavy hoofbeats. Through the veiling cottonwoods could be seen the ribbon of road, which cut across brown hillside and flat, two hundred or so yards from the stream.

"This notion that you had earlier, John? Of staging an ambush? Are you still holding it?"

He bit the words out as the horse loped on. "It's a helluva lot better than getting run down like rabbits by those coyotes. 'The best defense is a good offense,' a wise man once wrote."

"You're a reader, John Slocum? You keep continuing to amaze this poor girl. And after last night, I thought you'd never surprise me again."

The big man said nothing, but instead spurred the gray. The horse moved down into the concealment of a broad, brush-choked gully, beyond which loomed a ridge that offered the lofty position he sought. Slocum eased his Winchester from its boot behind his knee and rested it across his pommel, ready in case they encountered more riders in the next few minutes.

"I just heard brush crash over there!" hissed Nadine, her fingers digging into Slocum's chest.

He instantly reined into cover. "I heard it, too, Nadine. Hush a minute."

The second group of riders, when they came into view, trotted toward the first ones. Below the cutbank, screened by brush, Slocum and Nadine had the advantage of being able to see without being seen. At the edge of the stream, the two groups of riders met and mingled, horses' heads tossing and bridle chains clinking. Among the party Slocum recognized Garroway, senior—with his bushy black beard—and his less-imposing but equally dangerous son.

All the men were armed like manhunters. They were almost certainly after Slocum and Nadine.

Nadine whispered: "Can't you shoot the murdering preacher from here?"

"I could, if I wanted to get us killed," Slocum whispered back. "Those sidekicks, though, they'd be on us quicker than a spooked javelina—and we'd be caught, sure as hell. I don't want that."

The Garroways and the others continued to confer for quite a while, unheard over the intervening distance. Then with much hoof-trampling of the grassy bank, they wheeled and started off again.

"Looks like they're guessing we'd naturally make for town—which is where they want to keep us from getting to. See, they're covering the road. They know we haven't passed 'em, because we haven't had the time. They must've cut the trail we made this morning, but lost it again at the place we rode the rocky stream bottom. Glad I learned that trick, back in the days of the Indian wars."

"What now, John?"

He pointed. "Up there's the spot I'd like to see us at. A good line of fire on the road, which the Garroways are sure to come riding back up, sooner or later."

Slocum kicked Blue flame into motion, and they negotiated the defile, emerging on the far side of a low hill, out of sight of Garroway's bunch. Along here, cover was sparse and easy to see through, which meant crossing was a gamble. There was no other choice, however. Slocum kicked the horse into a high lope, and they started for the ridge.

And then they'd reached it and were forced to run along it for about a hundred yards unexpectedly, since on the far side they'd come to a previously unseen drop-off. Slocum ground his teeth, holding on to reins and rifle, feeling the woman's breasts jouncing as she hugged his swaying, jarring torso. Her long blown hair whipped about both their heads as they dropped into another stand of trees—this time junipers. Slocum brought them to another halt, to look and listen.

He didn't like what he found out: They'd been spotted from down below.

A bullet sang overhead—harmlessly, this time. But their enemies were on to him and Nadine, and while at extreme rifle range for the moment, they were closing rapidly. As

Slocum watched, the dozen riders split again into two groups, one pincering to the left, the other to he right, all horses moving at a gallop. Slocum slid from the saddle, helped Nadine down, then gave a sharp slap to the gray's rump, sending it downslope to safety on the far side.

"Nadine! You've got that spare Colt I gave you from the saddlebag?"

"Do I ever!"

"Let's dig-in back of yonder boulder pile." As he spoke, he was helping her hobble to the great, gray jumble of granite. "Unlimber the gun, but hold your fire, for now."

"Will we make it, John, with the element of surprise lost?"

"No sense crying over spilled milk, woman. Here come the Garroways. They're the ones we want, and they'll be in our gunsights quicker than a grasshopper can spit."

And such was the case. The horsemen kept galloping full tilt, and when they'd come within fifty yards or so, they opened up. Pistols and long guns were the weapons of choice, smoke clouds blooming like fluff balls in a gone-to-seed dandelion field. Slocum and Nadine opened up, too, and the big man found out she hadn't lied about her six-gun skill. He saw a big sorrel—*not* a horse ridden by either Garroway—go down, dead when it hit, skidding heavily. The rider bit the dirt and flopped about, but then jumped up again and fled on foot back the direction he'd come.

"Nice work," Slocum called. "Keep firing, gal! They're bound to quit in a minute and fall back!"

Slocum fired at the rider in the lead—a galoot aboard a buckskin—and saw the 200-grain bullet punch him from the saddle. Meanwhile, Nadine sent another horseman's battered slouch hat flying. And then—right out there in the open—Garroway's riders bunched to a halt behind their fallen *compadres*. For a few seconds they were a shouting, confused group, and then Tom Garroway reached down and hauled the injured man to flop across his mount's withers.

Then they all reined about and sped back down the slope and into tree shelter.

"Will they try another charge now?" Nadine was ejecting spent shells from her Peacemaker and then replacing them.

"Either that or just potshot at us for a spell." Slocum pulled his head down as shots began popping in the trees, sounding for the world like firecrackers on a Chinatown New Year's Day. "Keep your eyes peeled now," he told the woman.

"Look, John! They're charging!"

Slocum, edging his head up over the boulder, saw riders erupting from both sides of the cedar bosque. Phineas Garroway galloped among those on the left, while Tom led the other hard-riding contingent. Again puffs of smoke spouted from the muzzles of guns. The whine of bullets forced Slocum to duck. And yet he knew that he and Nadine needed to return fire, repel the fresh onslaught, reduce the foes' numbers, and—hopefully—pick off Parson Garroway.

"Start shooting, Nadine," he shouted. "Only, for God's sake, don't get picked off!"

Slocum, his Winchester's stock snug to his cheek, sighted on a rider pointing a Spencer carbine. He squeezed the trigger, and the man jerked crazily, as in his forehead there appeared a round, red, dime-size hole. The Spencer slipped from dead hands as the Garroway man hinged over, then catapulted from the back of his running bay.

Slocum fired at another combatant, but this time the target's horse shied, avoiding the bullet.

While this went on, Nadine's Colt was spitting lead. A gunman spun half-around in the saddle, yelped in pain, and clutched his shoulder: The blunt-nosed lead slug had hammered home. His wound gouting a crimson flow, the man reined his mount around and galloped in retreat.

All at once, the slope and ridge were quiet—eerily so. Slocum looked across at Nadine, who'd slouched back against a large chunk of sandstone, head down, hair loose and swinging, six-gun resting in skirt folds between her bent legs. Dust and gunpowder soot streaked her face, and her wrinkled dress was damp with sweat at the armpits and across the breasts.

She looked stricken by the heat radiating from the sun-blasted boulder pile, as well as from all the noise and shooting.

Slocum could see she wasn't used to fighting for her life like this.

He was kicking himself for not taking on Garroway's force single-handed, but of course, he and Nadine had been forced to share a horse, and they'd had bad luck in running into their enemies early on. Now, he knew, it was up to him to turn things around and get the preacher and his son, which hopefully would discourage the other gunmen.

As he hunkered down, reloading, he had a hunch—one telling him that he could improve his position. If Nadine and he weren't holed-up together, come the next assault they could have their foes in a deadly crossfire. "Nadine," he rasped, "see that low mound of ground there, under the ridge?"

"I see it."

"I'm taking a run on over there, and now's a good time to make my try. Here, swap your six-gun for my rifle—that way I won't be slowed down so much. When I'm in position and they come on their horses again, lay down the same kind of fire as before, trying to hit the Garroways. I'll be shooting, too, and we'll have a better chance at 'em."

She put on a brave smile. "I'm with you all the way, Slocum. Not only to save my own self and you, but to get revenge for cousin Fiona. Damn that phony parson!"

Slocum set off, racing up the hummock and throwing himself over it. When he hit the earth, he lost no time in rolling to a crouch, then peering warily back over the crest. He'd moved just in time. The enemy was emerging from the tree line down below again—but with a difference. Slocum sat up with a start, a Colt in either fist. As he squinted down at them, he could see their spread-out line of seven—and they were advancing on foot.

Uh-oh, he thought. Change of plan.

The men, walking and providing poorer targets, were able to dodge from outcrop to outcrop, and even take cover occasionally behind the horses that had been killed minutes earlier. Only two lagged behind on horseback, apparently waiting to see how things were going to go.

These were Phineas and Tom Garroway.

But the pack of attackers under their command was advancing, and Slocum knew not to let them close on Nadine, to take her in a rush. He reared up to shoot, the .44 belching, bucking in his fist. One of the men in the line squawked once, then sprawled on the ground. He was dead, Slocum reckoned: The shot had felt damned good as he tossed it.

Shots, and plenty of them, were now directed at Slocum, some zipping past his ears like hornets, others spanging stone and showering needle-sharp granite chips. From her position, Nadine was using the Winchester, levering and triggering repeatedly. Some of the jaspers fell back under her barrage, changed their minds, and ran over Slocum's way.

Phineas Garroway's force dodged swiftly up the gentle incline, shooting as they came, defying the hail of six-gun lead hurled down by Slocum. A brown-haired giant sporting a handlebar mustache went down screaming and kicking, his kneecap blown into a shower of blood and shredded ligaments. A more runty tough halted, opened his mouth, stared down in disbelief at his slug-pierced chest, then crumpled.

Slocum grinned wolfishly. He was experiencing the old,

familiar feeling, as if a half dozen cups of coffee were hitting his belly on a chill morning. His brain was clear as high-country air, his survival instincts honed as sharply as his trusty pocketknife.

Now he remained crouched behind the hummock, placing his shots carefully, trying to make each one count. He heard, "Attaway, boys—ventilate his damned carcass! Follow me!"

"We'll do 'er, Norm! Let's get the polecat!"

Norm ran up to vault the hummock, firing from the hip with a battered Henry carbine. Slocum, standing up, eared back the hammer of his left-hand six-gun and jerked the trigger. Norm took a wound that shattered his right collarbone, and, face squinched up in pain, he stumbled and lay thrashing.

Slocum spun. Another man was on him, dragoon pistol leveled, yelling a battle whoop. No time to recock and shoot! Slocum brought his Colt up and around, slammed the frame to the man's mouth, and felt teeth disintegrating. The man fell away, groaning in pain like the last few.

Phineas Garroway, a too-far pistol shot away from Slocum, sat on his chestnut gelding and bellowed orders. Slocum wanted the black-bearded man badly, wished him within reach. Then, suddenly, his wish was granted as, deciding his men needed help, the preacher waved his horseman son toward Slocum's hole-up. Then he put spurs to his own mount.

But: Plenty's wrong with the setup, Slocum thought. The preacher's got a scattergun, a goddamn double-barreled ten-gauge!

He saw the preacher's other sidekicks falling back, letting their leaders charge through.

Uh-oh, Slocum! he said to himself. Check-out time or buck the odds!

The Garroways, father and son, galloped straight on at him.

• • •

Tom Garroway wasn't bright, but he was young and strong and loyal: loyal to his old man, who didn't make him work, only fight. Who'd brought him to the point of shared ownership of a passel of prime land—if . . .

If they could silence for keeps the one who'd figured out their crimes: John Slocum.

Now Tom was galloping down on Slocum, who held two six-guns, one empty, the other partly so.

Slocum sighted and fired, and Tom saw his fathers' horse take a bullet, falter, go to its haunches, and career groundward.

"Get the son of a bitch, son! Get the son of a bitch!" The call was a rallying cry.

Seeing his father flipped clear of his dying mount, Tom maneuvered his dun gelding up to the standing man, crowding close, not letting him shoot. "Goddamn you, Slocum," the big kid heard himself holler, even as he dropped the hammer of his Smith & Wesson.

But he glimpsed Slocum in motion again, falling back, as the slug from the gun whipped through his sleeve. He didn't cry out, or dodge, even though Tom Garroway was following him with his .45. Instead he threw himself forward. Tom saw him collide with the spooked horse, felt his leg wrapped by his foe's strong hands.

Then he was dragged from the saddle, into Slocum's jaw-sledging fist.

Tom felt as if he'd been poleaxed in the lower face; the sky spun and went dark, fiery pinwheels spiraling in his brain. But then Tom's gaze cleared and he saw his enemy again: the tough, combative Slocum. So he waded in on this opponent, swinging wildly. Slocum sidestepped him by a hand's breadth, and then, his emptied six-guns abandoned and flung down, he lashed out with a punch that buried knuckles in Tom's midsection.

Tom was a tough egg, and came back from the blow,

hammering Slocum's temple with a rock he'd snatched from the ground. Slocum's knees folded, and when he fell, Tom leveled a tremendous kick to his torso.

With an authentic, Georgia-inspired Rebel yell, Slocum bounded up to resume the fight. From the corner of an eye he was aware of the older Garroway, but since Slocum had his hands full at the moment, he fixed full attention on big, brawling Tom. Tom circled Slocum like a veteran boxer, darting feints, then sharp, stinging blows to face, arms, chest.

Tom launched one of his most awkward swings yet, giving Slocum the chance he had been waiting for to drive a fist to his opponent's nose.

Tom saw the roundhouse blow coming, but could do nothing to dodge. Pain exploded downward to his chin, outward to his eyes. He loosed a howl of rage and agony.

At the same time, Tom heard a familiar voice shouting: "Slocum, stand back from my son! I'm warning you—"

Phineas Garroway's silver-chased, ten-gauge Greener— one of England's finest firearms—cut loose with a mighty boom.

A hole exploded in big Tom's midsection, and almost chewed in half by the load of buckshot, the young man tumbled backward, spilling a double handful of glistening intestines.

And numbing darkness took possession of his body and brain. . . .

Forever. . . .

"Jesus Christ! I've killed my own son! Blessed Jesus, help me! H-h-help . . . m-me . . ."

But the anguish in the preacher's cry failed to faze Slocum. He was beside Phineas Garroway in three quick strides, yanking the smoking shotgun from his trembling hands, breaking it open, and casting the unspent cartridge in the dirt. "Damn it, Garroway, pipe down. You killed a killer is all—even if he *was* your own flesh and blood, your son."

Phineas had thrown himself on the mangled and bloody corpse. Meanwhile, Slocum peered around and saw the last of the bodyguards hightailing it through the cedars.

And Slocum saw someone else: Nadine, who was hopping toward him as fast as she could, her lame leg dragging. She brandished Slocum's Winchester in the air and, forgetful of her discomfort, grinned. "We're alive, John! Oh, God, it feels good!"

"Slocum, you . . . you polecat!" bellowed Garroway, leaping up.

"Nadine! Whoa! Look out!" Slocum yelled. But Garroway, infuriated, ran at the woman and grabbed the rifle from her with a powerful jerk.

Oh, Christ, Slocum thought. But it was on *himself* that the preacher turned the weapon, ramming the barrel into his mouth and triggering the cocked Winchester with a long, uncalloused, extended middle finger.

The weapon roared out with a *crack!*

"My God!" shrieked the Macy woman.

The bullet sped up the Winchester's barrel, then into the insanely gaping mouth of Garroway, burrowing through tongue and palate. Then on upward it churned, through the brain. A millisecond later the top of the parson's skull blew off. He pitched to the side as if swept by a huge broom, then flattened on the ground in a grotesque sprawl, motionless.

"Is he finished, John?" said Nadine. "He must be!"

Slocum pulled the Winchester from the crimson muck. "You're right on that score, Nadine. Dead right."

And she was in his arms, trembling and sobbing some, but not all that much, really.

He was glad to be there, seeing it.

21

Nadine was talking as she and Slocum rode: "If I can get Fiona's will voided, John, I stand to get possession of the ranch, don't I? I *do* want it to belong to just me, not Joel. And John, there'll be a place for *you* on the spread, at first working for me—on account of what folks might say—but later a better arrangement! Permanent, for both our sakes! Oh, John, do I have plans!"

So saying, she waved the will she'd found in Garroway's pocket. The one she'd pronounced a forgery.

Reviving her hopes.

The couple were going now at a light trot, but this time not with them both aboard Blue Flame. The smiling Nadine had appropriated Tom's dun. Now they were bound for Antelope Creek, Slocum quietly listening, hearing elation in Nadine's voice.

He didn't share that elation, although he did feel tolerable. The Garroways done for—not a bad piece of work. Les Van Eaton would be informed, and the undertaker would be collecting the bodies.

In a few months, Slocum judged, the matter of ownership of the Diamond 7 would go on a court docket. Eventually there'd be a ruling, according to the laws of Colorado— and perhaps a jury's whim.

Slocum was a *trifle* curious: Would Nadine get the whole caboodle? Or would the surviving members of the congregation have a claim?

Might Nadine and the sodbusters wind up splitting the land?

The craziest notion of all: Would Cecil come out of the woodwork?

"So, you see, John, what I have in mind . . ."

He let her rattle on, scarcely listening.

Did he, Slocum, give a shit about the Diamond 7? Hardly. He had no interest in the job of foreman—or that of live-in stud. He was too used to being on his own, sometimes up and sometimes down, but always doing *what* he chose, *when* he chose. Answering to nobody.

The ranch partnership deal with Billy: That stood to be enough of a stretch for John Slocum. And he'd be giving it a try, in just a few more days . . .

Nadine had gone quiet. Then: "John, you're not even *considering* staying on the Diamond 7! Confess. Haven't I been wasting my words?"

The man stroked Blue Flame's neck, then shrugged.

"You told me you were heading someplace. Where?"

"Socorro, in New Mexico Territory. Near Wild Horse Butte. Pretty spot, good graze."

"John, I'm sure it's *very* pretty."

She wasn't mentioning all the fun they'd had in his bedroll last night—but she had to be recalling it. "Maybe someday a woman will steal your heart, John Slocum."

He let on he hadn't heard that last.

The buzzards were gathering far aloft—coasting, tiny cinders drifting in ever narrowing circles above the killing ground Slocum and Nadine had ridden from. Now some of the birds dropped behind the hills: always on duty when needed, always hungry.

Let them make the most of their meal, before the wagons rolled out from town.

Peering at the ridge line and the bright sky, Slocum tugged his hatbrim down to shade his eyes.

JAKE LOGAN

TODAY'S HOTTEST ACTION WESTERN!

__SLOCUM'S WAR (Giant Novel)	0-425-13273-0/$3.99
__SLOCUM AND THE BUSHWHACKERS #163	0-425-13401-6/$3.99
__SAN ANGELO SHOOTOUT #165	0-425-13508-X/$3.99
__BLOOD FEVER #166	0-425-13532-2/$3.99
__HELLTOWN TRAIL #167	0-425-13579-9/$3.99
__SHERIFF SLOCUM #168	0-425-13624-8/$3.99
__VIRGINIA CITY SHOWDOWN #169	0-425-13761-9/$3.99
__SLOCUM AND THE FORTY THIEVES #170	0-425-13797-X/$3.99
__POWDER RIVER MASSACRE #171	0-425-13665-5/$3.99
__SLOCUM AND THE TIN STAR SWINDLE #173	0-425-13811-9/$3.99
__SLOCUM AND THE NIGHTRIDERS #174	0-425-13839-9/$3.99
__REVENGE AT DEVILS TOWER #175	0-425-13904-2/$3.99
__SLOCUM AT OUTLAWS' HAVEN #176	0-425-13951-4/$3.99
__AMBUSH AT APACHE ROCKS #177	0-425-13981-6/$3.99
__HELL TO MIDNIGHT #178	0-425-14010-5/$3.99
__SLOCUM AND THE BUFFALO SOLDIERS #179	0-425-14050-4/$3.99
__SLOCUM AND THE PHANTOM GOLD #180	0-425-14100-4/$3.99
__GHOST TOWN #181	0-425-14128-4/$3.99
__SLOCUM & THE INVADERS #182	0-425-14182-9/$3.99
__SLOCUM AND THE MOUNTAIN OF GOLD #183	0-425-14231-0/$3.99
__SLOCUM AND THE COW TOWN KILL #184	0-425-14255-8/$3.99
__PIKES PEAK SHOOT-OUT #185 (Coming in July)	0-425-14294-9/$3.99

Payable in U.S. funds. No cash orders accepted. Postage & handling: $1.75 for one book, 75¢ for each additional. Maximum postage $5.50. Prices, postage and handling charges may change without notice. Visa, Amex, MasterCard call 1-800-788-6262, ext. 1, refer to ad # 202c

Or, check above books Bill my: ☐ Visa ☐ MasterCard ☐ Amex		
and send this order form to:		(expires)
The Berkley Publishing Group	Card#_____	
390 Murray Hill Pkwy., Dept. B		($15 minimum)
East Rutherford, NJ 07073	Signature_____	
Please allow 6 weeks for delivery.	Or enclosed is my: ☐ check ☐ money order	
Name_____	Book Total	$_____
Address_____	Postage & Handling	$_____
City_____	Applicable Sales Tax	$_____
	(NY, NJ, PA, CA, GST Can.)	
State/ZIP_____	Total Amount Due	$_____

If you enjoyed this book, subscribe now and get...

TWO FREE

A $7.00 VALUE–

If you would like to read more of the very best, most exciting, adventurous, action-packed Westerns being published today, you'll want to subscribe to True Value's Western Home Subscription Service.

Each month the editors of True Value will select the 6 very best Westerns from America's leading publishers for special readers like you. You'll be able to preview these new titles as soon as they are published, *FREE* for ten days with no obligation!

TWO FREE BOOKS

When you subscribe, we'll send you your first month's shipment of the newest and best 6 Westerns for you to preview. With your first shipment, two of these books will be yours as our introductory gift to you absolutely *FREE* (a $7.00 value), regardless of what you decide to do. If

you like them, as much as we think you will, keep all six books but pay for just 4 at the low subscriber rate of just $2.75 each. If you decide to return them, keep 2 of the titles as our gift. No obligation.

Special Subscriber Savings

When you become a True Value subscriber you'll save money several ways. First, all regular monthly selections will be billed at the low subscriber price of just $2.75 each. That's at least a savings of $4.50 each month below the publishers price. Second, there is never any shipping, handling or other hidden charges—*Free home delivery*. What's more there is no minimum number of books you must buy, you may return any selection for full credit and you can cancel your subscription at any time. A TRUE VALUE!

A special offer for people who enjoy reading the best Westerns published today.

WESTERNS!

NO OBLIGATION

Mail the coupon below

To start your subscription and receive 2 FREE WESTERNS, fill out the coupon below and mail it today. We'll send your first shipment which includes 2 FREE BOOKS as soon as we receive it.

Mail To: **True Value Home Subscription Services, Inc. P.O. Box 5235 120 Brighton Road, Clifton, New Jersey 07015-5235**

YES! I want to start reviewing the very best Westerns being published today. Send me my first shipment of 6 Westerns for me to preview FREE for 10 days. If I decide to keep them, I'll pay for just 4 of the books at the low subscriber price of $2.75 each; a total $11.00 (a $21.00 value). Then each month I'll receive the 6 newest and best Westerns to preview Free for 10 days. If I'm not satisfied I may return them within 10 days and owe nothing. Otherwise I'll be billed at the special low subscriber rate of $2.75 each; a total of $16.50 (at least a $21.00 value) and save $4.50 off the publishers price. There are never any shipping, handling or other hidden charges. I understand I am under no obligation to purchase any number of books and I can cancel my subscription at any time, no questions asked. In any case the 2 FREE books are mine to keep.

Name _____

Street Address _____ Apt. No. _____

City _____ State _____ Zip Code _____

Telephone _____

Signature _____
(if under 18 parent or guardian must sign)

Terms and prices subject to change. Orders subject
to acceptance by True Value Home Subscription
Services, Inc.

14255-8

By the acclaimed author of <u>Texas Legends</u>

GENE SHELTON

TEXAS HORSE TRADING CO.

Dave Willoughby is a Yankee gentleman; Brubs McCallan is a Rebel hellraiser. The unlikely partners met in a barroom brawl, and the only thing they have in common is a price on their heads—and high hopes for getting rich quick. The Texas frontier is full of wild mustangs waiting to be roped and sold. Too bad Dave and Brubs know nothing about catching mustangs...so why not just *steal* some horses?

__TEXAS HORSETRADING CO.   1-55773-989-7/$4.50
__HANGTREE PASS   0-7865-0019-0/$4.50
   (Available July 1994)

Payable in U.S. funds. No cash orders accepted. Postage & handling: $1.75 for one book, 75¢ for each additional. Maximum postage $5.50. Prices, postage and handling charges may change without notice. Visa, Amex, MasterCard call 1-800-788-6262, ext. 1, refer to ad # 485

Or, check above books and send this order form to: The Berkley Publishing Group 390 Murray Hill Pkwy., Dept. B East Rutherford, NJ 07073	Bill my: ☐ Visa ☐ MasterCard ☐ Amex (expires)
	Card#_____
	Signature_____ ($15 minimum)
Please allow 6 weeks for delivery.	Or enclosed is my: ☐ check ☐ money order
Name_____	Book Total $_____
Address_____	Postage & Handling $_____
City_____	Applicable Sales Tax $_____ (NY, NJ, PA, CA, GST Can.)
State/ZIP_____	Total Amount Due $_____